THE MYSTERY
AT
CHRISTMAS CASTLE

A Teddy and Pip Story

By Lisa Maddock

First published by Cavidae Press
Shakopee, Minnesota 55379

ISBN: 1978355025

This book is printed on acid-free paper.
This book is a work of fiction. Places, events, and situations in
this book are purely fictional and any resemblance to actual
persons, living or dead, is coincidental.

Printed in the United States of America.

For Allison

Also by Lisa Maddock

Teddy and Pip:

A Tale of Two Guinea Pigs
The Bridezilla Who Stole Christmas
The Trouble with Max
Nubb Trouble
The Case of the Halloween Spy
Teddy and Pip's Big Adventure

The Lucy Mackensie Series (age 12 and up):

Silver Linings Part One

Christmas is good when best friends are near.
I am happy Molly Jane is here.
Christmas is best when hats have bells.
Joy to the whole world, my heart swells!

Chapter One
A Christmas Miracle

It is my most favorite time of the whole year: Christmas. And it isn't only my most favorite time because I get presents. I like it for lots of other reasons too.

I can't know for sure what is going on in grown-ups' heads, but I do know there is a lot of work they have to do before Christmas. For them, it can be a time full of stress instead of peace and joy. But even though that extra work is going on, I think people get nicer and care about each other more at this time of the year. I think that is something to feel real happy about. Do you notice that too?

After Thanksgiving, I started thinking that another guinea pig party for my grandmas needed to happen soon. My grandmas love it so much when Teddy and Pip visit (and who can blame them?), and a Christmas guinea pig party sounded perfect to me.

Well, the idea turned into a bigger and bigger deal, and then it was not only Teddy and Pip coming, but every guinea pig I even knew of!

Mom said she already had seventeen zillion things of her own to get done, so if the party was going to be a big deal right before Christmas, I needed to do a lot of the work myself.

I totally agreed with her about that. And I agreed to work super hard on the party whenever I could get the time. It wasn't as easy as I thought to find time, because there was always homework and also piano to practice. So far, Mrs. Kelly hadn't given us a break with school stuff, and my piano teacher likes to do a piano Christmas concert in December. A person has to be ready for something like that, you know. Christmastime can be a busy time for kids, too.

Since the guinea pig party was my idea, I worked very hard on the decorations, cards, and all of the other details without any complaining. Of course, it turned out that I had lots of Mom's help. No matter how busy she is, she always finds time to help me out, especially when it is for a good cause. And after all that hard work, the party was happening today.

The rec room at Shady Acres hardly looked like itself, thanks to twinkling lights all over the place (thanks, Daddy!). Even the parakeet house had lights on top and also fake snow.

The big round tables looked perfect. Mom and Mrs. Sutter put red and green plastic cloths on them and also made centerpieces out of frosted cookies on fancy plates.

As soon as they sat down, every single grandma and grandpa at those four fancy tables had a sparkly Molly Fisher card in front of them. As people came in (with the help of Carlos), we quickly and sneakily addressed envelopes.

Yeah, there were *four tables* full of people! That is a lot more than only the grandmas in my club.

I wanted everyone who wanted to come to be able to, so we made enough spots for forty people. The Shady Acres helpers we talked to guessed that would be enough spots. But if even more people came, we were ready for that, too.

I was real glad that Shady Acres already had some Christmas going on before we showed up. Quiet music played in the background, and a really tall artificial tree was already decorated and lit up in the corner. It had the kind of lights that twinkle on and off and change color, too. I love those—don't you?

I felt so happy inside as I stood back and looked out at my party. All the tables were packed full . . . and wow! Now Mom was putting a cloth and cookies on table *five*!

I smiled and waved at my best friend. Nora was in charge of table one (with help from Hannah and Kaylie). Wipes were ready for "you know," and Nora's guinea pigs, Peanut and Coco, were sniffing cutely around the table. They let people pet them and give them treats, too. I don't mean cookies—no way! The guinea pigs had healthy treats only, like lettuce and celery and pieces of red peppers and stuff.

Since I was in charge, I decided we would move one of Nora's guinea pigs to the new table. Either Kaylie or Hannah could be in charge. Or, probably, both. I was about to zoom over there to tell Nora the new plan, but I didn't need to. She read my mind, like best friends can do, even from way across the room. I watched her get right on it and gave her a thumbs-up when our eyes met up.

Sophie and her Coco were in charge of table two. Max was there next to his girlfriend, grinning like he does whenever she is nearby.

My new friend Penny and her guinea pig, Sammie, sat at table three. Penny's mom was there too with Grandma Lucy, who is Penny's relative.

I bet you can guess who was at table four, right? Yep—Wally and Amelia with Teddy and Pip. Oh my gosh, the guys were *so* cute today! Amelia found them new jingly Christmas hats: white and blue knitted stocking caps with a white puff on top. When they walked, the hidden-inside jingly bells jingle-jangled adorably. Can you imagine it? (Tee hee!)

Sophie and I had made red jingle hats (just like Teddy and Pip's from last year) for all the other guinea pigs to wear. So far it didn't look like they were staying on. Oh well. It's easier to pet a guinea pig when he or she doesn't have a hat on anyway. We could get them all on later, just long enough for Max's amazing, adorable video and the group guinea pig pictures.

When Wally checked in with me a little while ago, he said Pip was being awesome. He had not slipped up one bit so far. In case you don't know what that means, Pip not slipping up meant he didn't do any talking or singing in front of people.

Yeah, Teddy and Pip can talk. And sing. If this is the first book of ours that you've read, that will be a shock, I'm sure. It is an amazing thing that has made my life cuckoo (in a good way) for a while. Read the other books for the details.

I actually did see Pip's little mouth moving along to a Christmas song once or twice. But he can't even help it. I mean, it is so hard for Pip to not sing!

I watched Teddy do his cute little circle dance in front of Grandma Pearl. After he did his circle one way and then the other way, he let each grandma pet him, if she wanted to, while he had a treat. (Teddy is so sweet!)

Sassy Pip went from person to person, getting his little face in each of theirs, then saying a loud *"WHEEEE!"* That is his new thing. It might make some people a little nervous, but most people seem to like it, especially kids.

Their litter box was under Wally's chair. He and Amelia keep track of when the guys need to "go" with their own special signals. When they are at home and can talk, they just tell someone that they need to go. But when they have to be regular guinea pigs and protect the secret, they do two wheeks, or two whoops, or something like that to let Wally and Amelia know.

The Shady Acres workers and other grown-ups were moving around the room like experts, making sure the human party guests had whatever they needed. Mom and Aunt Patty paid special attention to Nanna (who was at Sophie and Max's table). Nanna is their grandma and my great-grandma. For some reason, Nanna is not a fan of animals. I don't think it is because of allergies, but maybe it is. I don't know. All I know is she did not hold a guinea pig during the whole party and was very fine with that. She was happy to enjoy the rest of the fun stuff, like bingo and word scrambles and treats.

The only thing that would've made this party all the way perfect would've been snow falling outside the big windows. But, darn it, no dice on that. There was only more of that cold rain we'd been having, which was making even more messy mud in Westerfield.

I have to admit that I got jealous of my cousins in Wisconsin who had two feet of snow on the ground already. They had even gotten a snow day! In case you don't live somewhere that gets snow, that means they got to stay home and make snowmen and stuff instead of going to school because school got closed up. (Cool, huh?)

I even watched the weather on TV a little bit with Daddy last night. I saw some snow on the map that was not so far away from where we live. It didn't look very far at all on the TV map—only a couple inches away. I keep hoping the wind will blow it down here so we will need a snow day too.

I stopped by the parakeet house again before going back to my important and tricky job of pouring red punch. So far, I hadn't spilled very much at all (yay me!). The parakeets weren't getting much attention during this big guinea pig party, and I felt bad about that. "Hi, guys!" I said. "How are you cuties doing?"

All of a sudden, I could tell I wasn't standing alone anymore. When I turned my head, that confusing boy Benny Nubb was standing right next to me.

He didn't say anything for a long time. He just stood there, like he does. Then he finally said, "Well?" at me and rolled his eyeballs around.

I stared at him and stared at him. "Well, what?"

"Well, I brung him."

"Brought," I said without even thinking about it first. I am always fixing that kid's bad grammar for him. "Brought who?"

And then that confusing kid pulled a hamster ball right out of his big jacket and showed it to me.

I felt a total shock wave, let me tell you, because there was Frank the hamster, at Shady Acres on my party day. Poor little Frank was trying super hard to run in his ball, but he couldn't get anywhere with the ball held real tight in Benny Nubb's hands.

"You—? But . . ."

"You said I should bring him here." Uh oh, now Benny Nubb sounded like he was getting upset with me. (By the way, this actually was our usual way of having a talk.)

"I know I did. I just didn't think you would actually . . ." I had said that to him when we were sort of arguing about something else on the bus the other day. I said he should do something nice for someone, for a Christmas miracle, instead of being mean to little kids. Like, why not bring Frank to the party I was doing at Shady Acres? I sure didn't think he heard me or would do it in a zillion years!

But there he was, taking my advice or suggestions. Wow.

"I'm glad you came," I had to admit out loud. "Thanks."

He shrugged and looked around the room a bit. "Guinea pigs," he said snortily. I couldn't tell if he actually had grumpy thoughts or not when he said that. Benny Nubb actually *does* like guinea pigs. He just sometimes forgets that I totally know that.

"Penny's here with Sammie," I said. "Why don't you and Frank join her table?"

Nothing.

"If everyone watches out for him, Frank can run around in his ball, right on the table, I think. Don't you think?"

Benny Nubb shrugged some more, like he usually does for an answer to everything.

"I'll move the cookies out of the middle," I offered.

He shrugged even more. Then he dropped his jacket right there on the floor. Then he stomped over toward Penny's group. "Hey, Benny!" I called after him. It felt weird to do that. It always sounds super weird to me to say his actual name out loud.

He stopped stomping and turned back to look at me with squinty eyes.

I gave him a thumbs-up that I think maybe made him almost smile at me a little.

Mrs. Sutter was already moving the cookies, so I stayed right where I was and watched for a while. Penny's table got all excited about seeing a new pet. They even clapped a little at Frank's cute running in his ball.

Sammie didn't seem too interested in the hamster ball, and I hoped he wasn't upset about Frank taking some of his attention. I watched for a bit more until I saw Sammie seeming pretty happy to be cuddled by Grandma Rose. Whew.

Wow. What a miracle.

Chapter Two
A Surprise About Amelia's Surprise Getaway

It was a peaceful time in our living room. Music was playing inside, it was dark outside, and our perfect tree was all lit up. All of this was especially great with glorious Christmas in our not-far-away futures.

Tweets was out and in the room with me, but I was keeping him safely away from the tree like I promised. Birds can't chew on or eat pine needles. I am not sure if Tweets knows that or not, but he is pretty smart, so he probably does.

He and I were in the middle of our very own made-up Scrabble game on the coffee table. This is how it goes: I make a row of seven letters for him and put it on the little wooden Scrabble shelf. I have my own set of seven letters on my shelf. When I set him down, Tweets picks a tile for me by tapping it with his beak. I need to watch real closely to see which one he taps first, because he likes to tap them all . . . or knock them over and stuff. Actually, after the first tap, I need to take his tiles away so he stops knocking them around. After that, I hold him on my finger or let him sit on my head while it's my turn. If I don't keep him busy, he pushes the letters around on the board, too.

Sometimes I wonder if he is finding a new way to give me information or clues, you know? Like using Scrabble letters. Wouldn't that be cool?

Anyway, the first letter Tweets taps on has to be the first letter of the next word I make. Get it? Except for that part, I play the game the regular way. Oh, also expect for keeping score. If I can't make a word on the board, he gets a point. If I do, I get a point. Believe it or not, Tweets almost always wins this game. He was winning this time, too. Not because I can't make up good words, but because he keeps picking real hard letters for me, like Q and X.

When the doorbell rang, Tweets headed right to the kitchen with a loud *"SCREEEECH!"* My parakeet is not a big fan of the doorbell.

Mom was busy in the kitchen, making dinner out of all kinds of things I am not so sure about (like onions and celery and other vegetables and roast beef). I was a little nervous about how that would all turn out. Don't tell her, but I would've been happier to have her or Daddy dial up some pizza. "Molly?" she called, wanting me to get the door. "Peek out the window to see who it is first!"

After I peeked, I knew it was Wally and opened the door right up. Since we had just seen him at Shady Acres, I was surprised to see him again—and maybe a little worried, too. For one thing, using the front door was fancy and formal. Usually, Wally comes in the side door. Also usually, he has a box of guinea pigs with him. This time, he was there by himself.

"Hello, Miss Molly!"

"Hi, Wally. Did you come for dinner?" I joked. "I have no idea what it is, but there are lots of vegetables getting chopped up in there. Including onions."

Wally chuckled like he does and shook his head. "I hope I have not interrupted a meal."

"Nope. Whatever it is, it's still getting cooked, and Daddy isn't even home yet. What's up? Is something wrong?"

"No, no," Wally said as he took off his shoes and set them on the mat by the door. He took off his coat, too. This was not going to be a quick visit. "Nothing is wrong, I promise," he said. "But I do need to speak to all of you."

Mom called, "Who is it, Molly?" from the kitchen.

"It's Wally!" I yelled back, and then I waved him after me. "Sorry. I hope I didn't hurt your eardrums."

He chuckled and rubbed both ears a little bit. "I am only teasing," he added. "All is well, my friend."

Even though Wally (Professor Walter Holmby) is a college teacher of economics and stuff, he is most of all our friend. That means we don't have to be fancy around him. We can let him come right in the kitchen, even when Mom is making dinner and Tweets is out. It is even okay with Mom for Wally to sit right at the table. Hardly any company does that when Mom is cooking—not even Amelia. We have come a long way from when we first met Wally, believe me.

"Wally! Hello!" Mom set down her big knife (what a relief!) and wiped off her hands. "What can we do for you?" She offered him coffee and also a bunch of other things, but Wally didn't want anything except to talk. "How are the plans coming along for your anniversary surprise?"

"Ah. Well," Wally sighed.

Those two were enough words for Mom to stop smiling and look worried instead. "Oh dear. Don't tell me things have fallen through."

"Fallen through?" I gasped. "Things can't fall through! Max and I have big plans for Teddy and Pip while he's watching them!"

Wally fingered his mustache a bit. "Not fallen through," he said. "But . . . for one thing, it is not a surprise anymore. I could no longer keep this from Amelia. I spoke to her about it in detail this evening."

"Didn't she like your idea?" I asked.

Mom gave me a look like I was interrupting too much and getting on some thin ice, like I sometimes do.

"Oh, no, no—she liked it just fine," Wally chuckled. "She was thrilled, in fact. This particular B&B is a place which holds dear childhood memories for my wife."

Mom and I waited for him to explain the problem to us, because so far it seemed like there wasn't one.

"Amelia is quite excited to go. However . . ."

Mom and I waited some more.

Then Tweets said a really loud *"HELLO?!"* which made the room less tense.

Wally chuckled and said "hello" back before he said, "The truth is, it would simply be too difficult for her—for both of us, honestly—to leave the boys at Christmastime," he finally said.

I sighed and said, "Oh. Right," but Mom didn't say anything.

"I am afraid that leaving them behind would lessen the enjoyment of our getaway."

I could tell Mom was trying hard not to frown or have an attitude about that stuff. She does not understand one bit about Teddy and Pip or how anyone could feel like that about guinea pigs. Especially not those two. Teddy, Pip, and my mom still have some big issues to work out.

"And so, unfortunately," Wally went on, "that means we must choose between canceling, postponing . . . or bringing them along."

Mom made a clicking sound with her tongue and then turned back to her chopping.

"Of course, we all know how much those two do not like change in any form. Taking them along could prove to be tricky," he said.

"Oh, Wally," Mom sighed. I guess she just couldn't keep quiet. She set down her knife again. "Surely you can find a way to have your romantic getaway and also . . . accommodate . . . them."

"Well, yes, I actually believe so." Wally was looking a little bit nervous now, which was not his usual look. He had an idea that my mom wasn't going to be real thrilled about. "There is one solution that has come to mind which involves . . . the three of you. It is asking a lot, so feel free to refuse," he ended quickly.

Mom and I just sat there, waiting. I was totally excited and she was probably full of dread.

But then Daddy came bursting into the kitchen, interrupting and breaking the spell. "Mmm! Smells *great* in here! What's for dinner?" he asked, like he always does. Daddy totally has dinner on his mind after a day of working. He gave Mom a kiss and me a big hug before he even noticed Wally. "Oh! Hi," he said to Wally. "Sorry, Wally—didn't see you there!"

"Hello, Dan." Wally tipped his head at my dad, like he does, and then apologized again for being at our house at dinnertime.

Daddy said the same stuff Mom did and even invited him to join us. After all that, Wally got back to what he came to ask for.

But that was exactly when Tweets decided to stop spying on us from the ceiling fan. With a big *SQUEEEEECH!* he flew off of the fan and landed right on Wally's head.

Oh my gosh. I couldn't help the giggles, even though it made my mom horrified.

"Goodness," was all Wally said. He was totally surprised because Tweets had never done that to him before.

Before any of us could figure out the best way to solve the weird problem, Tweets flew off Wally's head again and landed on the windowsill instead.

Yay! Tweets on the windowsill means Morse code. Sometimes. It had been a long time since he'd done that, and I was excited to know what he had on his smart birdie mind.

Nora and I were real excited about having the whole break to do fun stuff, like solve a mystery. And maybe here it was! I knew it would make her super happy (and also less jealous of Penny) to be my partner in crime-solving.

I got out my sheet of codes that I keep right by Tweets' cage all the time and paid close attention. I won't do the details of the taps this time, if it's okay with you. Trust me on this: what Tweets tapped out were the letters *P* and then *O*.

When he was done, he flew on my head and bobbed around like he does. Then he said *"HELLO?!"* at me, like I wasn't getting it and needed to catch up.

"Molly?" Mom said through her teeth. "I think Tweets needs to be back in now. Don't you?"

I didn't, actually. Poor Tweets. One strike and he's back in instead of out. I gave him a special treat and said, "I heard you," in a whisper. "*P* and *O*. I'll keep my eyes and ears open for the mystery! Thanks!"

"HELLO, PRETTY!"

I kissed his little beak through the bars and then got back to my spot at the table.

Wally had a look on his face and his eyeballs on my bird. I was pretty sure that his thoughts were not about Tweets landing on his head, but about the clue.

"Yeah. You just heard him do Morse code," I said.

"Amazing," Wally said.

"I know it!"

"So!" Mom interrupted. "We were talking about your getaway . . . ?"

"Yes, of course," Wally said. "Well, as you know, I have reserved four nights at a bed and breakfast, up north a ways. This is a place where Amelia and her family spent many happy times when she was your age, Miss Molly. Though it is generally for more than one family, I have reserved the whole place for us."

My first thought was that it was weird to think of Amelia being my age, but also that we already knew about all this. Wally had told us his idea a while ago, at this very table. He was all excited because he knew his wife would totally love it. Back then, he'd asked me to stop in to visit Teddy and Pip while Max was staying over. I agreed to visit as much as possible.

It seemed like he was trying to make us agree all over again that the trip was a good idea.

"It is guaranteed that there will be snow," he said next.

"Lucky!" I couldn't help saying back.

Wally smiled. "I have been checking daily and there are at least two feet accumulated. More is predicted."

"Cool!"

"But not in the form of a storm of any kind," he added, looking at Mom now.

Mom nodded slowly.

"The internet and cell reception are not great," Wally said, looking sorry about that, "but there is better reception in the little village if that is needed." Wally looked at Daddy then moved his eyeballs back to Mom. "The shopping area is very quaint and full of . . . you know . . . jewelry and knickknacks and scarves and . . . such."

Mom's eyes sparkled for him about that, but Daddy only nodded seriously, like he felt sorry for Wally about that part of his anniversary trip.

Wally did a little cough and smoothed his hair and mustache. "Unfortunately, naturally, if we did bring the boys, we could never leave them alone in that house. The caretaker comes in and brings food and tidies up and so on at her discretion. And, so, there would really be no opportunity for shopping, or exploring the village, or much of anything else outside of the house, for the two of us, together, alone."

I had a feeling I knew what was coming next. Wally wanted me to come too. He wanted to hire me to be Teddy and Pip's watcher so he and Amelia could go to that village to shop for knickknacks and scarves sometimes.

I was super excited about it, but also kinda not. Let me explain. I guess I felt like Teddy and Pip probably felt about it all. It made me sad to think of leaving my mom and dad right after Christmas. Plus, I would miss being in my house, which was full of awesome decorations—and Tweets. And my presents. And time with Nora. And don't tell Nora, but I had some plans planned out with Penny, too.

Feeling a little nervous now, I tuned back in to what Wally was saying. "This is, perhaps, hopefully, where the three of you could come in. If you would agree. I know it is asking a lot."

Mom closed up the oven after she checked on that roast thing she was making. She looked at Daddy, whose eyes had gotten wider.

"The house truly is large enough that you could have a room quite far from the boys," Wally surprisingly said toward Daddy.

Daddy blinked his wide eyes a few times real fast.

"Miss Molly would have her own room too, and the downstairs is *very* spacious."

"You want *all* of us to come with you?" I gasped. "Me, Mom, and Daddy, too?"

Wally nodded a bit nervously. He was asking a lot, he thought, and was worried about the answer. "I would absolutely guarantee a relaxing and scenic experience for you. And you would surely enjoy those shops," he aimed at my mom. "You and Amelia, perhaps, could do that together?"

Mom nodded very slowly, like it wasn't quite exactly a "yes" so far.

"I have been assured that one television set is tucked away upstairs and is working, though in general, the house is geared toward reading and relaxing."

I'm sure Daddy was thinking hard about hardly any TV, and also the internet and cell phones being not so great.

I waited, holding my breath, until l needed to stop that and take another one.

"The idea is that we could trade off minding Teddy and Pip—myself, Amelia, and Miss Molly, so that all would get to enjoy time outside of the house. We would never ask Molly to be in charge of them for more than a couple of hours at a time—and never at night. All is paid for. You would be our guests. And the caretaker is known to be a marvelous cook." Wally folded his hands, unfolded them, and then folded them up again. "If it is too much to ask, I do understand. It is rather last-minute."

Mom's mouth was moving, but no sounds came out. Daddy was confusingly frowning a little but also nodding a little.

"It is a three-hour drive," Wally said, sounding sorry about that part. "But, as I said, it is guaranteed to be scenic toward the end. And there are no storms

colors. She finished her bracelet up and, not a big surprise, gave it to me. "I'll miss you, that's all."

"I know. Me too. But Hannah and Kaylie aren't going anywhere. And you could call Penny," I tried, but no dice. Nora was not ready to call Penny a friend so far. "I promise to call you when I can figure out how to get a good phone signal. I'll have Daddy help me with that."

"Okay."

"Don't be sad. 'Tis the season to be jolly!" I said, which made her laugh. I studied the bracelet Nora had just made for me and decided it was really great. I told her so. "You are super crafty!"

"Thanks, Molly." After we shared a big best-friends smile, Nora wanted to go right back to the subject that was upsetting her again. "So explain to me again why you are going on a trip with your almost-neighbors, who you see all the time, right after Christmas, when it is for their anniversary. Anniversaries are about lovey-dovey mushy stuff, usually. I think."

Of course, as usual, I couldn't really explain all the way. If Nora goes on a trip, even if it's a long one, she doesn't worry about leaving Peanut and Coco. She asks someone (usually me) to stop by and feed them twice a day and to spend time with them a little bit. She couldn't imagine that it would be a big worry for grown-ups to leave their guinea pigs for a few days.

It is a hard thing to have a big secret from your best friend. But it is also super important to never tell her, or anyone, that Teddy and Pip can talk. Fourth-grade girls have a hard time keeping secrets, for one thing, and I would not want to make Nora's life harder. If people, like scientists, find out about the talking, Teddy and Pip could end up in a research place. That would be horrible.

"Teddy and Pip are totally sweet and awesome, as you know," is what I said. "And that means that Wally and Amelia can't really go off somewhere alone together very much and also feel all the way happy about it."

"Yeah, but—"

"I hate leaving Tweets, too," I added.

"Why can't you bring Tweets?"

It was a fair question, but the answer (that Teddy and Pip were real scared of Tweets for no good reason) would not make sense to Nora—or to anyone who didn't know they could talk.

Mom walked in with some cookies for us before I could say whatever I was going to say. I was glad for her timing. Plus I was glad about the cookies.

Even though she had already made a zillion batches for the family Christmases, Mom baked even more for the trip and as a "thank you" for Mrs. Sutter.

"Nora, please tell your mother I say thanks again for stopping by to water the tree and bring in the mail."

"Sure, Mrs. Fisher. And thank you for the cookies!"

"I am sending home two dozen for your family," Mom said.

Nora said "yay!" about that, and then Mom got her distracted some more by asking about the bracelets and liking them a lot.

Before long, Mrs. Sutter was calling and it was time for my friend to leave for dinner.

"I'll call you soon!" I promised.

"You'd better!"

"I will. *P* and *O*!" I reminded her in her ear. "Keep your eyes and ears open!"

Chapter Four
Off We Go, in Search of Snow!

I don't know about you, but I like car trips a lot. This one was especially fun because we were heading to a place we'd never been before. That meant there were new things to see and make games out of, which is awesome. And, best of all, we were heading out of a not-snowy place and toward a very snowy one.

Wally had called up and told us that it was a for-sure about the snow, so we'd better bring boots, hats, mittens, and warm coats! Yay!

In the beginning, most of the driving was on what Daddy calls the "turnpike," which sounds like a fish to me. Anyway, that part was not super exciting, but I ate cookies while we played the license plate game, and that was fun. I found a total of twenty-two states, which was pretty cool. Lots of people were driving around on our side of the country right now.

After we gave up on the other twenty-eight states, we played an alphabet game. You know, like *A* is for *automobile*, *B* is for *bumper sticker*. The rule is that it has to be something you see, like a thing, and not a word on a sign. Daddy tries to cheat sometimes and use words on signs instead. But that is a whole other game. Anyway, I love doing that stuff, and Mom does too. She is super good at it.

"But nothing starts with *Q*," Daddy said. "I mean, except queens and quails, and we won't see any of those off the interstate. . . ."

"We can use signs for *Q*," I said, like I always say after we try for at least a little while. "And it doesn't have to even be the first letter. Same for *X*."

"Thank you, Molly," Daddy said.

We made it all the way through (with special rules for hard letters) except for *Z*. Then we took a break and just looked at scenery.

"How much longer?" I couldn't even help asking. We had been off the big highway a long time and were driving on winding woodsy roads now. It was starting to get dark outside, so I got to see Christmas lights twinkling from every single snowy house. It was also snowing real lightly, adding to the ton of snow already on the ground!

I could hardly wait to get out and drop down in that snow and make an angel, or a snowball, or a snowman, or all of them.

"Another twenty minutes," Mom said. "Isn't it lovely here?"

"Yes!" I agreed. Since I didn't want to miss anything, I wiped away the fog on my window so I could see better. Some boys were finishing up a huge snowman, and I saw a big skating pond too, right in a person's yard. The pond was lit up with big lights, and people were skating around and around. "It's like a winter wonderland here!"

Mom suddenly said, "Oh, Dan, look! That must be the village Wally told us about! We're getting really close, Mol!"

"Yay!"

Daddy said, "Hmmm," and that was probably about the shopping village. Daddy is not a huge fan of shopping.

The village was very cute. It was all lit up with lights and was . . . old-fashioned, I guess. Like, I expected to see horses and buggies instead of cars parked there. I am not a big shopping fan either, actually, but it did look like a great place to do that, if you had to. "Are you gonna get a bunch of new scarves?" I asked Mom.

She laughed a little and said there were other things to look at too besides scarves.

"Knickknacks, right?"

"Right. And lots of other things too."

The village's church had a really tall steeple—and also pretty windows that matched the Christmas lights—and really looked like a puzzle my grandpa did last year.

"Are we almost there?" I asked again. Now that we were so close, it was getting really hard to wait.

Daddy chuckled at me while he shook his head. But it turned out that he was not shaking his head because he was saying "no." He made a turn, and then we drove along a snowy driveway, winding through lots of tall trees. "Think you can you wait two more minutes?" he asked.

"Only two more minutes?!" We were so close . . . and then I knew for sure we were there when I saw Wally's little car, topped with fluffy white snow, parked near the garage. "There's Wally's car! This is it!"

Mom said, "Oh my!" as the big blue house came into our windshield view. It looked almost exactly like the picture we'd seen on the computer.

"Wow," I whispered. It was pretty dark outside now, but the lights coming from the windows— including that cool princess tower—looked extra magical because of that. A lit-up Christmas tree with colored lights was set up right outside on the front porch, just like in the pictures. I had never seen that before in my neighborhood. There was also a big green wreath on the front door. "So cool," I whispered.

Wally popped out of the house and waved Daddy into the empty garage. He had nicely saved the inside spot for us and left his own car out in the snow. That's just the way Wally is: super nice.

I could see Amelia waving from a window with a guinea pig in her arms. It was Teddy. I waved back like crazy, and then I zipped up my jacket and put on my mittens. I was so excited that I was totally bouncing in my seat! I opened the door as soon as Daddy was all the way parked. "Can I go in? Is it okay if I go inside to see the guys?"

"Go ahead, kiddo," Daddy laughed at me. "We'll bring in the stuff."

I got out of the car and then out of the garage, and then I jumped right into some snow and flopped down. I made a quick angel like I'd planned to and then tested the snow for stickiness. It was pretty good quality, I thought. Like, tomorrow, a really good snowman would probably happen.

"Take off your boots before you step on the rugs or carpet!" Mom called after me.

"Okay!" I zoomed right at Wally, and after I gave him a hug that made him say "oomph," I kept going toward the front door and that pretty lit-up on-the-porch Christmas tree.

Out of the corner of my eye, I couldn't help noticing a girl standing real still in front of a little house nearby. The house was a matching blue and had its own colored lights and a smaller wreath on the door. The little porch's lights were on, and I could see that the girl was watching every step I took with a big frown on her face. Her arms were crossed up real tight, too. Her frown got even bigger at me. Then she turned around and went into that little house. When she gave the door a slam, the wreath flopped around like crazy.

I had been a little bit worried that this rented vacation house would not have any Christmas inside. I knew it would look great outside because of the pictures I'd already seen, but you really never knew about the inside of places. We went somewhere after Christmas once before when I was younger, and that's how it was: no tree, no lights, no nothing. It was a fun time, don't get me wrong, but it was like Christmas went *poof* on me.

Well, this place definitely had Christmas going on! It was like a Christmas explosion had happened in there! The room I walked into was a big but cozy living room with an old-fashioned fireplace flaming away. There were cushy chairs next to the fire and old-fashioned rugs covered the wooden floor. There were green garlands draped over stuff all around the room and sparkly lights were mixed into those too. In front of the big front window was a big, decorated (real, not fake) Christmas tree that smelled awesome. There were even presents under it! (But Amelia told me later that they were just for decoration.)

Anyway, everywhere I looked in that big room, I got to see something cheery and red or green. Christmas had for sure not gone *poof* on me. It had gone *kaboom!* instead.

"Molly Jane is here!" Teddy squeaked. *"Nice day, Molly Jane? Nice weather?"*

"Hi, Teddy! Hi, cutie! I *LOVE* the weather! Hi, Amelia!"

"Hello, Molly."

"Um, did Mom Jane stay at her house and not come here with you and Dad Dan? Please tell us that she did not come to this place where we are at, Molly Jane, okay?" Teddy whispered at me.

"Teddy!" Amelia shook her head and held a finger up to her lips. "Please remember what we talked about, Theodore. My goodness! The Fishers are here as our guests and are very kind to come all this way to help us out."

"Amelia, we talked much also of not wanting to be at this very place one bit. Remember that thing? But here we are anyway. And maybe we are here anyway with Mom Jane, too, and that is not very okay or what we prefer."

"Teddy, my dear one, we are all friends here," Amelia said. "And Jane is to be treated only with respect. She has not done a single thing to you—"

"Except for she put us in a bucket. What about that thing?"

"Once. Long ago. And not for unkind reasons."

"Not for good reasons also or either, Amelia, who I love."

"Hush now, they'll be in soon. Have courage and be kind, Teddy. Have courage and be kind."

"Where's Pip?" I asked, because it was a surprise not to hear his complaining added in with Teddy's.

"HERE IS PIP! PIP IS HERE! PIP HAD TO DO HIS POTTY AND NOW IS DONE WITH THAT! MOLLY JANE, WE WOULD LIKE TO GO HOME NOW, TEDDY AND ME. WE DO NOT LIKE IT HERE. LET'S GO! THIS AMELIA, WHO WE LOVE, IS NOT LISTENING VERY MUCH TO OUR SCREAMING ABOUT THAT STUFF. OR WALLY MUCH EITHER. NO GOOD! HOME IS WHAT WE PREFER!"

"True. We truly do not like it here," Teddy agreed. *"There is nothing to do or see. There is only just snow and snow and snow, white and white and white, and we want to leave now. Thank you."*

"LET'S GO!! MOLLY JANE SAVES THE DAY! THANK YOU! ORRIE VWAH, AMELIA!"

Amelia had probably heard this stuff seventeen zillion times already. She shook her head with a smile as she handed Teddy to me so she could scoop up Pip. She whispered something into Pip's little ear that made him seem happy again. Then she kissed his nose and said, "Don't forget!" She put Pip in the travel cage, which was set up on top of a little table by the side window. Then she nodded at me because she wanted me to put Teddy in there too.

I was not surprised when both of them started complaining about this idea. *"NO GOOD! THERE IS NO FUN IN THIS LITTLE TRAVEL CAGE OR ANY TREATS! WORST OF TIMES IS THIS THING! I WOULD LIKE TO GO BACK TO OUR GOOD HOUSE WITH FREEDOM AND WALKWAY! I WOULD LIKE TO GO NOW OR SOONER!"*

"Now or sooner!" Teddy agreed. *"Thank you!"*

Amelia only put a finger on her lips and said *shh* at them as the front door opened.

Wally and my parents were carrying lots of stuff. And even though they all had their hands and arms full, I knew that was not even everything we packed. I mean, the car and trunk were totally full. There was barely room for me in the back seat.

Wally really wanted to help bring in the rest of our things, and Amelia promised to open and close doors for everyone. It seemed like one of those times when the nicest thing a kid could do was stay out of the way. So I headed over to talk to the guys.

"This is so great," I said. "All of us together in a pretty, decorated-up house, with snow outside and Christmas all over the place!"

But Teddy and Pip were going to be grumpy. Not much can change their minds when they get like that. They didn't say anything. They just sat there, staring at me.

"Aren't you glad you can talk all you want here, like, most of the time?"

They stared some more. Then Pip said, *"EXCEPT NO TALKING WHEN HAIR-TAKER IS HERE. WHICH IS NO GOOD."*

"Aww, guys," I sighed. "Can't you give this place a chance, for Wally and Amelia? Couldn't you do it as a special present for their anniversary? Because they are your best friends and you love them? That would be the best present ever from you two, I think. Couldn't you pretend to not be unhappy?"

"There is nothing to like here. There is nothing to do."

"NO CHANCE! WE CANNOT GIVE IT! WE DO NOT DO THAT STUFF! MOLLY JANE, WHAT ARE YOU SAYING ABOUT PRETEND?!"

Wally had set down his load from Daddy's car and was shaking his head at the guinea pigs. "My dear fellows," he chuckled, "we are going to have *such* a terrific time here—whether you are able to admit it or not."

"We won't."

"NOPE!"

"For one thing, there will be fun games to play all together—"

"Except for we don't like that stuff."

"NO GAMES! NOT FUN!"

"—like charades," Wally went on.

"We do not like that stuff. What is 'sure aids'? That sounds no fun."

"NO NO NO! WE DON'T LIKE IT! WE WON'T DO IT! WALLY, WHAT ARE YOU EVEN SAYING TO US?!"

"And all best friends together—"

"*Except that Max is not here and also not the pretty and smart Sophie. That means not all best friends are here, Wally.*" Teddy scratched an ear with a back foot. "*And yes, I surely know that the Sophie is not in the Best Friends Club, because she does not know of our secret. Those beans are not spilled so far.*"

"*PIP DOES NOT SPILL BEANS! STOP SAYING HE DOES!*"

"*But we love her and she is not here and that is sad.*"

"*WE ARE LEAVNG NOW! GOODBYE, WALLY!*" Pip squeaked. "*ORRIE VWAH, TOO! MOLLY JANE, TAKE US AWAY!*"

"Oh, my dear fellows," Wally sighed and laughed at the same time. "Surely you can and will come up with something that you do like about this adventure. Eventually. Will you please, please, for me, give it a try? For Amelia, too?"

"*WE LOVE AMELIA!*"

"*Wally, we will try, but the thing of that thing is that you and Amelia will do dating here in this snowy-snow-snow place without all best friends. You will leave Pip and me all alone in this surely haunted house, which is full of monsters, and we will be alone. Alone with no TV and nothing to do and no reading or food or water and no best friends. Except maybe Mom Jane, and she will surely find a bucket to put us in.*"

"*TEDDY IS RIGHT! THAT WILL SURELY HAPPEN TO US!*"

Wally said a chuckling "incorrect" about all of that.

"Wally, I know it will be like that. It will be. It will be sad."

"No, it will not," Wally said, and then he picked up his pile of our stuff and headed for the tall, winding stairs.

"WE WOULD LIKE TO GO BACK TO OUR OWN PERFECT HOUSE!" Pip yelled again. *"THIS HOUSE IS NO GOOD!"*

Even though it seemed impossible to get them to cheer up, I decided to try anyway. "I have some great ideas too," I said. "Really fun ideas! You just wait and see."

"It won't be fun. We want to go home. There is no walkway here, and we will be stepped on or will be stuck in this small travel house here for days and days. We will be bored. We will not get to explore. It will not be fun. Monsters will probably eat us."

"PIP HAS NO HIT SINGLES IN HIS VERY ROCK STAR HEAD, MOLLY JANE! THE HOUSE IS EATING THEM ALL UP! CRUNCHY CRUNCH! NO GOOD! THE FANS WANT HITS!"

"They'll come to you," I said. "Be patient."

"THEY WON'T! I CAN'T!"

"And I know you will have a lot of fun. I am going to make sure of it."

"Molly Jane, how is it that you are going to make sure of it?"

"Well, for one thing, you two are going to help me solve a mystery." I hadn't meant to say that. It just slipped out. "Would you like to do that?"

"But we are afraid of mysteries. I think. And also especially of monsters. And other things. Teddy

will think about it, but do not think the answer is 'yes.' We would prefer to go home."

"WELL . . . PIP IS A ROCK STAR. HE CAN ALSO SAVE THE DAY AND DOES THAT MANY TIMES. BEFORE. BUT HE IS MAYBE NOT A DUDE WHO DOES . . . WHAT DID YOU SAY, MOLLY JANE?"

"Solve mysteries?"

"NO! PIP DOES NOT DO IT!"

"I think there might be a mystery to solve at this house. Tweets gave me a clue—"

"DO NOT SPEAK OF THAT BIRD! EEK EEK, SCARY BEAK!"

"Molly Jane, please say to us that the claw-foot bird is not here in this haunted house! Please say he will not peck our ears and scare us out of our little heads!"

"Tweets is staying with Max. He is very far away. Which is sad. I miss him."

"MAX IS A DUDE WHO SHOULD BE HERE WITH HIS BEST FRIENDS! THAT IS THE SAD!"

"What is this mystery you are speaking of? Teddy is thinking it is too scary and maybe it is not what he wants to do."

"Well, solving a mystery is figuring something out that is confusing."

The guinea pigs stared at me.

"Remember when the red bird was tapping on your window?"

"WE REMEMBER. IT WAS NO GOOD! TAPPING, CLICKING MONSTERS! CHICKEN TOWELS! EEK EEK! THERE ARE MONSTERS IN

THIS HOUSE TOO?! IS THAT WHAT YOU ARE
SAYING, MOLLY JANE?!"

"No, that isn't one bit what I'm saying. Don't
you remember that the tapping turned out to *not* be
monsters?"

*"But Pip and me were very sure that thing was
monsters tapping and clicking and also crunching. It
was not a good time that we want to remember. Or
to have happen all over again."*

"The point is, I solved the case—me and some
helpers. We found out that the tapping was only an
outside bird—who could never hurt you. And then you
didn't have to be afraid anymore. Remember that?"

Nothing.

"That's what solving mysteries is like. Also,
remember the first mystery we had together? The one
you asked me to solve? When Wally and Amelia's
postcards got stolen?"

*"NO-GOOD BARBARA STOLE OUR
POSTCARDS! SHE DOES NOT LIKE GUINEA PIGS!!
DO NOT TALK ABOUT THAT PERSON TO US NOW
OR EVER! DO NOT SAY THAT BAD BARBARA IS
HIDING IN THIS HAUNTED HOUSE AND WILL
TAP AND CLICK AND ALSO TAKE THINGS FROM
OUR AMELIA AND WALLY! DO NOT SAY IT!"*

"You guys are totally looking for trouble, aren't
you?"

*"We are not looking, but we are finding it. Or
it is maybe finding us."*

"Barbara isn't anywhere close. I promise. We
are, like, two hundred miles away from Westerfield
right now, and that's real far."

"BUT BAD BARBARA CAN DRIVE A CAR, PROBABLY, AND SHE CAN COME HERE! SURELY SHE CAN!"

"Except that Wally wouldn't let anyone come here who didn't love you guys. No way."

"Except Mom Jane . . ."

"MOM JANE IS HERE!"

"Please think about helping with the mystery, okay? For me? And please think about at least pretending to be happy for Wally and Amelia."

Amelia showed up carrying the guys' special bowls full of salad. That, as usual, no matter what, made them very distracted. Instead of using words, they started up whoops and wheeks like regular guinea pigs.

After she gave them the veggies, Amelia set two guinea pig sleeping bags in the travel cage too. Both were totally furry inside and were made out of Christmas cloth. One had candy canes all over it and white fur inside and the other had Christmas bulbs and was red inside.

"I wish I had one of those," I joked.

Amelia smiled. "Aren't they wonderful? I found these online. So perfect for cozy cold-weather napping. I'll see if they make one big enough for a ten-year-old detective girl."

I said, "Cool!" even though she was kidding.

While the guys got busy eating, Amelia headed for one of the cushy chairs by the fireplace. She waved me after her. But then she said, "Oh! One moment!" and left me there by myself.

I studied the tree and as many ornaments as I had time to study until she came back. This time, she had a cup of tea for herself and a Santa mug of hot chocolate for me (with whipped cream on top *and* chocolate sprinkles. Yum!). Amelia likes to have tea with me and talk like I am a grown-up too.

We sat there totally enjoying ourselves while the rest of the grown-ups finished unloading and getting settled. But I figured that since Amelia was in charge, it must've been okay to do that.

"How's it really going with . . . ?" I nodded my head a little bit toward Teddy and Pip, who were still munching and mumbling away in their travel cage.

Amelia smiled as she shook her head. "They are still adjusting. But I have lots of hope for them now that you are here."

"I'll help as much as I can," I said. "That's a promise."

"I know you will. It was a good idea to arrive last night when they were both sleepy and willing to curl up and not make a fuss. But today has been a different story. They have voiced their complaints in every way they know how to—including in French."

I laughed. "Yeah, I heard some of that."

"Oh, we are so grateful that you are here!"

"Well, I love the snow, and this place is so pretty. I mean, I don't think it'll be anything but fun." I sipped my hot chocolate (and burned my tongue a little).

"Oh, isn't it lovely?" Amelia sighed. "Has Wally explained to you that I came here often as a young girl?"

I nodded and then blew real hard on my hot chocolate.

Amelia studied me a bit, probably noticing my questions and seeing a mystery. "I'm afraid I don't recall."

"Do you think they used to live in here, the girl and her family, but now they can't anymore?" That could explain why she was so grouchy. Maybe she likes big houses a lot better than small ones.

"Perhaps," Amelia said slowly. "I suppose that is possible. Sometimes places like this are closed to guests at certain times of the year and the family lives there for a while."

"It could make a person grouchy if she thought other people were pushing her out of a house that she really liked, right?"

Amelia did a little nod.

"And then she had to live in a tiny house instead. And her mom had to cook for and clean up after people."

Amelia nodded a bit more and said, "It could. Perhaps you two can introduce yourselves if you see her around?"

I said, "Hmm," about that, which is not the same as saying "yes" or "no." The real truth was that I had no plans or hopes to see that girl ever again.

"I understand that the girl's father is currently working overseas somewhere," Amelia added. "I would imagine that is very difficult for a young girl—especially one who also just lost her grandmother." She kept her eyes on her tea and the Christmas tree after she said that stuff so I wouldn't feel too bad about what she maybe thought I had just been thinking.

I did feel kinda bad for what I'd thought about the girl. It didn't make me want to see her again, but I did feel sorry for her. "Yeah, that would be real hard. I don't even like it when Daddy has to go to the city for a day. And losing a grandma?" I did a shudder.

Amelia nodded.

"Even though I kind of have a lot of them, it would be super sad to lose any of them, especially a relative."

"I bet there will be an opportunity for you girls to chat over the next few days," Amelia said with a smile. "I'm sure you can make her feel better. If anyone can, it's Molly Jane Fisher."

I said, "Yep," but I wasn't so sure I meant that. Amelia is a very nice lady, but she doesn't totally understand how kids can be and act, I don't think. There was a better chance that, while we were staying at Christmas Castle, for both of our sakes, that girl and I would only stay away from each other a whole lot.

Chapter Five
Dinner Games

Mom and Daddy were all done putting things away upstairs. Being settled made Mom feel much better. She doesn't like to not be settled. They wanted me to check out my room, and I really wanted to check it out too. I thanked Amelia for the cocoa, put my cup on a Christmas coaster, and then zoomed up the curvy staircase ahead of my parents.

Then I had to wait at the top for them to catch up. Parents don't zoom up curvy staircases—or anywhere, really, very much. I forget that sometimes when I get excited.

"This one is yours." Mom pointed at a white door with a little flowery board on it. On the board was a name: "Elizabeth." *Elizabeth Danby, of course! Evelyn's friend from being a teenager.* "We are right next door," Mom said next, showing me their door too.

It was good to see how close they would be to me. Even though I'm brave about most stuff, I like to have my parents close when I am in a totally new place like this.

The name of their room actually wasn't anybody's name; it was only called "Suite Two." So that was too bad.

I went into Elizabeth's room and looked all around me. It was definitely old-fashioned, but not in a bad way. I mean, it was really nice. The wooden floor was covered up by a big wooly green rug, and the curtains were heavy and red—for Christmas, I bet. I mean, I bet they changed that stuff up when it was a different season. The quilt on the bed was green, red, and white too, and best of all, there was a canopy over it! I have always wanted to try a bed like that.

I had an old-fashioned bathroom of my very own, and I even had my own little Christmas tree! It wasn't a real one like the one on the porch or downstairs, but it was very pretty and all lit-up just for me. "This is so great!" I called. "I love my room!"

Mom came in and we had a hug. "This really is a nice old house," she said. "And I am glad we came. Now that we're here and settled."

(Told ya!)

"Is my stuff in the closet and drawers?" I asked, even though I knew it totally was.

She opened up a drawer and then the closet door to show me. "Your things are in the bathroom, too."

The closet wasn't big like closets in new houses were. I mean, in newer houses you can walk right into closets. You can even sit in there and play, if you want, or you can play hide and seek or whatever. This closet looked real small from the outside, but it turned out to be long and winding, going way back and out of sight.

It actually seemed like a maybe-creepy tunnel. I wondered how far back it went and what was at the end of it all. I thought about it and thought about it—and then I needed my dad to check it out with a flashlight, or else I wouldn't be able to sleep tonight.

Daddy found a flashlight and then squished his way back into the closet for me. He walked as far as he could go. "The ceiling gets lower and lower back here," he called. "It's slanted. But at the end, about five feet from the turn, it's a solid wall, Mol. Nothing to worry about."

"Are you sure?" I had to ask. "It's a solid wall? Like, totally solid?"

Daddy kissed my forehead when he got out. Then said he was totally sure it was totally solid. He also said we could keep our bedroom doors open for just in case I started thinking more about the closet and got worried at night. He left the flashlight for me too.

I started feeling better about the creepy closet, and then I decided, "I'll bring Teddy and Pip in here tomorrow. They can explore it with me, even back in the low area where you couldn't fit, Daddy."

Daddy said, "Sounds good," but Mom made a little face like she always does whenever the subject we are talking about is Teddy and Pip.

"Come check out our room," she said. "It's very nice. We even have an old-fashioned clawfoot tub!"

"Clawfoot sounds scary, not nice," I giggled.

"You silly," Mom said, messing up my hair. "Always looking for trouble, aren't you?"

I looked over their room and decided it was very nice too. The bed was frilly and white with a furry red blanket on top. Their rug, like mine, was green. The best thing was that their room was not so very far away from mine. I checked out their closet and decided that it was not scary at all. They, luckily, had two small closets instead of one bigger one. And no secret tunnels.

Daddy had already found the one TV in the house and was busy flipping channels. "The reception sure isn't great. But I suppose I'll still be able to catch the game," he said, which made Mom's eyeballs roll around.

"It's nice to get away from screens for a few days," she said. "To enjoy nature and books and good company instead. Plus a little shopping."

"I agree," I said. "Except maybe not too much shopping."

"Wally and Amelia have some games in mind to keep us entertained after dinner," she said. "I wonder what that will be like."

"Not real normal," I said, "if Teddy and Pip are part of it. So be ready!"

Mom shook her head, but she was smiling anyway. "I will be."

You guys probably don't want to hear a lot about the fancy table and the big dinner, am I right? It was totally like that: fancy and good. But the real fun was having Teddy and Pip right there in that room with us. I have spent a lot of time with those cuties, but never at a fancy dinner table.

They had decided to stop complaining for a while, which was a big relief. Either they were pretending to be happy or they had decided to be happy for real. I would have to ask later. Either way, they were being cute and funny, which made at least three of us at the table very happy.

The travel cage was closest to Wally's spot (and farthest from Daddy's) at that fancy table. Wally gave Teddy and Pip bits of salad, which made them very happy (and a little quieter, some of the time).

While we were eating more seriously, Pip decided to play with his favorite new present (a plastic ball that jingle-jangled when he pushed it with his nose). Teddy curled up in his furry guinea-sack and took a little nap with only his adorable face sticking out.

When we played a word game during dessert, the guys decided that they totally wanted to play too, never mind what they had said before about not wanting to.

"Something good to eat that starts with the letter . . . *B*!" Amelia said.

So far, we had done three other letters about three other things. Even though there were only five of us humans, it took a long time to get around the table because of our two tough judges.

Here's how *B* went:

Mom: "Butterscotch ice cream."

"ICE CREAM IS NO GOOD, MOM JANE!"

"Humans eat much of that stuff, but it is not good for them or for their teeth. Veggies are good, even for Mom Jane. Do not say that sweety-sweet stuff. Try again."

Mom: "Bread and butter."

"WRONG! PLUS DO NOT SAY THE THING OF BUCKET OR PUT US IN ONE!"

"Bread and butter is still not veggies. But we will let you pass. This time. Try harder next time. Tee hee!"

Every time it was Mom's turn, the guinea pigs gave her a very hard time (in a really funny way). Mom put her face in her hands, but I could tell she was actually laughing.

Amazing, huh?

Daddy: "Bratwurst."

"WHAT IS THAT THING, O-DADDY-O DADDY-O?! IT SOUNDS NO GOOD, SO I OBJECT! TRY AGAIN!"

Daddy: "How about beer, then?"

"NO NO! NO GOOD! NO NO NO!"

"Dad Dan, you are being a silly! Beer is not a good thing to eat. It is only for drinking at silly times! Our Wally does not like that stuff, and you should not either. Say something else!"

"WRONG!"

Daddy (laughing): "Baked beans?"

"BEANS?! DID YOU SAY BEANS?! WRONG WRONG WRONG! BEANS ARE FOR SPILLING, BUT PIP DOES NOT DO THAT THING! THEY ARE NOT FOR EATING!"

"Dad Dan, you silly! Pip surely spills beans. That is what happens with those things. Beans are not for you to like to eat. Say something else! Tee hee hee!"

Daddy: "Barbecued ribs."

"WHAT?! WHAT ARE YOU SAYING, DADDY-O?! YOU SAY WRONG THINGS AGAIN AND AGAIN! WHAT IS THAT STUFF? IS IT DUDE FOOD?! PIP IS

A DUDE BUT DOES NOT KNOW WHAT THAT STUFF IS ABOUT!"

Wally: "Boys, let us allow Dan his many answers and move along, okay?"

"Okay, Wally. But it is much fun to say 'no' and 'wrong' to Dad Dan. And also to Mom Jane. Nice day, Mom Jane? Nice weather, Daddy-o?"

"OBJECTION! WE ARE HAVING FUN WITH THAT DUDE! WE DO NOT WANT TO MOVE ON SO FAR!"

Wally: "Moving on. Brussel sprouts."

"Good job, Wally, my friend, for saying the thing of a veggie! We approve! Good job! No objections!"

"BEST OF TIMES! ROLY-POLY SPROUTS OF GREEN! PIP PIP HOORAY! OUR WALLY KNOWS OF THE RIGHT THINGS TO EAT AND SAY!"

Amelia: something that sounded like "bool-ya-base."

(I know! What in the world is that?)

"Tee hee!"

"FUNNY FUNNY! AMELIA MAKES A JOKE, RIGHT?! TEE HEE! THAT IS NOT A FOOD OR ANY OTHER THING. SAY SOMETHING ELSE, AMELIA! TEE HEE! YOU ARE BEING WRONG LIKE MOM JANE!"

Amelia explained that it was a soup or stew full of veggies and other things. The guinea pigs stared at her for a while. Then they both shrugged.

"MOLLY JANE?! WHAT IS YOUR ANSWER ABOUT B? SAY IT FAST! WE DO NOT HAVE ALL DAY!"

Me: "Bacon!"

"*Molly Jane, that stuff is for big men, not for a girl who is our Molly Jane. You need to eat broccoli or maybe berries. That is what Teddy says for food that starts with the B!*"

"Good job, Theodore!" Wally chuckled.

"*BROCCOLI, BERRIES, BANANAS—PIP PIP PIP PIP PIP PIP PIP IS MEEEEE! THE END! WE WILL NOT DO THIS GAME-THING ANYMORE. PIP WANTS TO DO ANOTHER SOMETHING!*"

Amelia held up her wine glass with a big smile. "Thank you, Jane, Dan, and Molly, for being here and making this a perfect trip. You are such good friends."

"A toast! All best friends together!" Wally agreed, holding up his glass too.

"*EXCEPT FOR MAX IS NOT HERE!*"

Everyone laughed when Pip said that. Then we all drank a toast with whatever was in our glasses (I had grape juice in mine).

"*TOASTY TOASTING! TEE HEE! CRUNCHY CRUNCH!*"

"*Except, friends, toast is not a drink; it is a crunchy food instead,*" Teddy said.

Pip suddenly stamped his little paw and yelled in his squeaky way, "*PIP IS NOW DONE WITH SILLY STUFF AND ALSO DONE WITH TOASTY TOASTING!*"

"Well then, what is it that you would you like to do instead, Pippen?" Wally chuckled. "Is it time to head for bed?"

"*BED? NO NO! IT IS NOT TIME FOR THAT, YOU SILLY! I WILL NOW TELL YOU WHAT PIP WANTS TO DO, WALLY FRIEND. THANK YOU FOR ASKING.*"

"You are welcome, my friend. Thank you for the nice manners—toward the end."

"YOU ARE WELCOME FOR MY NICE MANNERS, WALLY. HERE IS WHAT I WANT TO SAY: PIP DID MUCH BIG THINKING AND IS DECIDING NOW THAT HE WILL HELP MOLLY JANE WITH HER MYSTERY IN THIS PROBABLY HAUNTED HOUSE. THE END."

Every grown-up eyeball moved to me after Pip said that.

Mom said, "Molly?" in a nervous voice. "What is this about?"

"Nothing. I mean, it's for pretend," was all I could come up with in a hurry. "For fun."

"NO NO! MOLLY JANE IS SAYING THINGS THAT ARE NOT TRUE! MYSTERY IS TRUE AND NOT FUN! PIP IS READY TO DO THIS THING AND SAVE THE DAY, NOT ONLY JUST HAVE FUN! FUN IS NO FUN! WHAT ARE YOU SAYING, MOLLY JANE?!"

Teddy gave Pip a little shove and said, *"We will do the pretend mystery with our Molly Jane. For fun. That is what we will do. Never mind this Pip for now. Friends, you can do more games, if you would like, and Teddy will be your judge. Do the letter of L, okay? Yummy treats starting with that letter. Give good answers this time, okay? Teddy says lettuce— yum yum yum! Now go go go!"*

Chapter Six
Checking in with Nora

"Look, guys, don't get mad at my mom—" Whoops, that was a bad way to start this talk.

"MOM JANE—!"

"Pip, shush! We do not know so far what this talk with Molly Jane is all about. Maybe it is not about buckets or any other bad thing. We do not know so far why we are not to be mad at Mom Jane, or what she did for Molly Jane to say that thing to us. Be quiet for now. Maybe be quiet later, too."

"BUT MOM JANE—!

"Shush."

"Thanks, Teddy." I looked right into Pip's adorable little face and could tell he was working very hard not to keep complaining. "I want to tell you why I said what I said about the mystery."

"MOLLY JANE SAYS IT IS NOT FOR REAL BUT ONLY FOR FUN! WORST OF TIMES!"

"Yeah. I know. But I didn't totally mean that. See, grown-ups don't think a kid should go looking for a mystery to solve," I said. "They think it ends up being trouble. And they're kind of right."

"TROUBLE TROUBLE, BUBBLE BUBBLE!"

"*But Molly Jane, you are a detective girl. You do that stuff. It is what you do.*"

"Yeah, it is, but . . ." I looked at Teddy and then back at Pip. "It's different to look for the mystery instead of knowing there is one and solving it. And especially in someone else's house, like this one." I waited for objections, but they both only looked at me. "It makes grown-ups nervous," I added. "It's about privacy and stuff. Grown-up humans like privacy kind of a lot. You guys like privacy too. It's important to you that nobody learns your secret, for one good example."

"*That is truth.*"

"*PIP DOES NOT WANT TO DO RESEARCH!*"

"Anyway, that's why my mom wants me to be careful with mysteries. It's mostly about privacy."

"*And also about scary clicking monsters?*" Teddy guessed. "*Mom Jane does not want monsters to come to click at Molly Jane, who she loves?*"

"*MONSTERS?! PIP, TOO, DOES NOT WANT THAT STUFF!*"

"Hey now, don't start talking like that again. There are no monsters in this house. Or anywhere. Okay?" I pet them both for a while. Then I talked more quietly. "I am still going to look for a mystery for us to solve. I am sure there is one. If it isn't here, then there's one at home. And I am really super glad that you two are going to be brave and help me solve it, whatever it is. We just need to only talk about it like it's for fun now—until it's for real. Okay?"

"*WHAT ARE YOU SAYING, MOLLY JANE?! YOU ARE MAKING NO SENSE!*" Pip squeaked. "*TALK SENSE!*"

"Molly Jane, I will explain the stuff to this Pip for you. Teddy thinks he knows what you are saying. Some. Maybe. We will start the for-fun mystery thing after the darkly time is done. Now our friend will make a big promise about no monsters or bad guys. Yes? Vader is for surely not here in this blue house doing a mystery, right? And also not 'Don't Say the Name'? Right, Molly Jane?"

"Of course not! There are no such things as monsters, guys. Those bad guys are only in stories. There are only friends here in this house—"

"And also Mom Jane."

"MOM JANE IS NOT A FRIEND!" Pip got quieter when he saw my parents walk by the doorway. *"BUT MOM JANE IS NOT A MONSTER AND DOES NOT CLICK AND TAP. OR OTHER THINGS LIKE THAT. PIP WILL SAVE THE DAY ABOUT THE MYSTERY FOR YOU, MOLLY JANE,"* he whispered. *"WHEN YOU FIND IT. THE MYSTERY IS SNEAKY SNEAKING. PIP THINKS. MAYBE."*

"I'm proud of you guys for giving this place a try for Wally and Amelia."

"I LOVE AMELIA!"

"We are doing the try, Molly Jane. We do not want to be only complaining. It is not so fun as we thought it would surely be. We will do the games and say nice things instead. And maybe we will not only and always be in this teeny tiny travel cage with no adventures."

"I will make sure you have some adventure," I said. "We'll start tomorrow."

"PIP WILL WRITE HIT SINGLES IN THE MORNING LIGHT TIME. THEY ARE COMING, SO BE READY, MOLLY JANE!"

"I will be," I promised.

"ALSO, PIP WILL STOP THE CRIMES AND GET BAD GUYS. HE BROUGHT HIS VERY BLASTER TO THIS PLACE, MOLLY JANE, BUT DO NOT SAY THAT THING TO WALLY, OKAY? OKAY. BEW BEW! PIP IS NOT AFRAID. I DON'T THINK. FOR NOW. BUT NO 'DON'T SAY THE NAME,' OKAY?"

"Of course not, like I already said. Okay, guys— here comes Wally." I held a finger to my lips. "Thanks. Good night! I love you!"

Daddy's phone test showed us that the best spot in the house for making a not-crackly call was in the living room near the Christmas tree. Which is awesome, but weird. I don't know why a tree makes a phone call better, but that was the way it was at Christmas Castle. It is part of the "charm" here. I guess it is charming that we can't be on the phone all the time. People come to a place like this to get away from computers and phones and TV. That makes sense to me, too. I mean, if all you want to do is stare at a phone or computer or TV, you might as well stay home, right?

So anyway, while Daddy did his testing and called work, I got ready for bed. Then I went downstairs again and dialed up Nora's number in the special spot.

"I can't hear you very well," she complained, right in the middle of me trying to get her all caught up about the trip. I had just told her that Amelia named the house Christmas Castle when she was a little kid and wrote stories about it, too. "You keep getting crackly and stuff."

"Sorry. It's a cool house, but a bad phone place. Phones don't work here very well, but we get lots of charm instead."

"Huh?"

"Can you hear me now?"

"Yes! Stay *right* where you are. Like, don't move one bit."

"That's not as easy as you think," I said. "But I'll try." I held as still as I could. "Anyway, so I still haven't figured out what Tweets' clue means. I am really thinking I should call up Max and ask him to listen for other Morse code letters for me. Because maybe Tweets added some more and it's like a word scramble now."

"A word scramble? Wouldn't that be so amazing?!"

But then I thought about the bad phone crackles and how I was at a place where I wasn't supposed to be on the phone a lot anyway. "Um, maybe *you* can call Max for me . . . ?"

"Me?!"

"I mean, this place has bad phone service compared to at home. Like you were just complaining about to me. Remember?"

"Yeah, but . . ."

"Aww, come on! You know my cousin. You've talked to him before. It wouldn't be weird or scary. Would you this for me, best friend?" I gave her Max's phone number, real slow, and then I made her tell it back to me.

Nora was nervous about it, I could tell, but she did agree to do it. Whew.

And now I owed her a big favor.

"Maybe that is the clue that will get things going for me. I haven't figured out anything at all yet, as far as a mystery around here."

"Here either. I am keeping my eyes and ears open, though, like I said I would," Nora said.

"There are no *P* or *O* things or people anywhere in this house so far—or anything fishy about the people who are around here. Nothing fishy that starts with those two letters, anyway."

"So there is something fishy? Something that doesn't start with *P* or *O*?"

"Yeah, but not mystery-fishy."

"What?"

"There is a not-friendly girl who lives next door." I told her about the caretaker's daughter (whose name is Jess; Wally told me that at dinner). But then I had to add what Amelia told me about her sad life.

Nora was quiet for a while. Then she had to admit, "I feel sorry for her."

"Yeah. Me too," I admitted back.

"Are you *sure* Tweets did *P* and *O*?"

"Totally sure. He did it at least ten times."

"Anything else?"

"Well, maybe. But it isn't really a mystery. It's just a weird thing."

"A weird thing?"

"It's about Amelia's scary sister and a friend she had here a million years ago. Her name is Elizabeth, so don't get too excited. Amelia's sister is called Evelyn. I'm sleeping in that girl's old room."

"Huh. Well, it isn't going to be easy to solve a mystery when you can't even figure out what it is yet," Nora said (which was not very helpful).

"Molly?" Mom called from upstairs.

"Oh, that's Mom calling. I gotta go to bed. I'll talk to you tomorrow, best friend!"

"Okay. Promise you'll call!"

"I promise! Don't forget to call Max!"

Chapter Seven
The Second Day

I am not usually excited about breakfast. I always like lunch better. But I could hardly help liking breakfast today. Rosalie, who is Jess's mom and the caretaker at Christmas Castle, set stuff on the fancy dining room table and then left before any of us even saw her in the morning. There were warm muffins (including chocolate chip!) and scrambled eggs with lots of cheese, perfectly toasted toast, bacon, and orange juice without that pulp in it. There was also a bowl of fruit on the table and . . . well, that's enough talk about food, right? I need to get going on the mystery or you guys will stop reading this book.

Wally and Amelia had plans for after breakfast to go into the town for shopping in the shops. They needed a couple hours for that, and then they would be back for the rest of the day. For those two shopping hours, I was in charge of Teddy and Pip.

"It's okay to explore different parts of the house with them," Amelia said. "Just have their litter box nearby, and—here." She handed me a weird-looking cloth thing, sort of like a backpack (except weirder).

"What is it?"

She popped it over her head to show me. "It's for carrying the boys," she said. "It is a baby carrier that we have made alterations to. What do you think?"

I imagined Teddy and Pip snuggled into the carrier pockets and couldn't help giggling. "Oh my *gosh*, that is so cool, Amelia! You and Wally have the best ideas!"

"Wear it in front, like this," she said with a smile. "And Teddy and Pip can snuggle in these two specially made pockets."

I giggled some more when I tried it on.

"Oh, I have to be honest with you, Molly." Now Amelia did a little sigh. "They don't like it."

"Uh oh."

"But they also don't dislike it so *very* much."

"How much do they not like it?" I asked.

Amelia only made her eyes a bit wider for an answer. "We believe it is better and safer to strap them into this carrier and to hear the complaints than to carry them up too many stairs without it."

"Yeah. And I bet they'll learn to love it."

Amelia lifted up her eyebrows real high. Then she said, "Anyway, the boys can play anywhere in the house, except for the basement. I don't think any of us are allowed down there."

"Don't worry, I don't want to go down there either."

"The kitchen is fine, as long as Rosalie isn't in there working. But she shouldn't be back until much later on. That means you don't have to worry about the secret. The boys can talk all they want."

"What about that tower at the very top of the house?" I asked. "I am super curious about that place."

"I am curious too," Amelia admitted. "It was such a lovely and fun playroom when I was little!"

"Really?" I smiled. "Do you think I could bring the guys up there?"

With a little shrug and a smile, she said, "As far as I know, we have the run of the place—unless a door is locked. Some bedroom doors are going to be locked because Rosalie would rather not need to clean them if they are not going to be used."

"Okay. So as long as the tower room isn't locked, I can go in there?"

"If you can stand the complaints as you climb up all of those stairs with the boys, enjoy! Perhaps you will find some interesting toys up there for them to play with."

Wally appeared with a big smile and Amelia's warm jacket, which he handed to her. "Thank you for watching the boys for us, Miss Molly. I hope they are no trouble. Or not much trouble."

"Don't worry one bit. We are going to have a ton of fun!" I said. "Where are they?"

"They are finishing up their second breakfast in the dining room," Wally chuckled.

"What if they ask for a third one?"

He chuckled some more and then said, "Well, it's fine, I suppose. I surely hope that they do not trouble you by begging for treats the entire time we are out."

"Hey—Wally? What is the last name of the people who own this house?" I asked.

"That would be *Ellington*," he said without missing a single heartbeat.

Amelia snapped her fingers and said "right" about that, like she had forgotten and now she remembered again. "I was trying to remember so I could tell Molly."

"Are you sure?" I sighed.

"Yes, I am sure," Wally said while Amelia nodded.

"And the caretaker has that last name too?"

"Rosalie is an Ellington by marriage."

"And that's spelled with *E*, right?"

"Correct." Wally twinkled his eyes at me as he handed Amelia her mittens.

"Lots of *E*'s going on around here," I mumbled. "And not one single *P* or *O*."

"Not so far," Wally said nicely.

"I think Tweets is doing a word scramble, even though he has never done that to me before. He never gives me wrong clues."

Wally looked kind of amazed as he zipped up his jacket, his head shaking back and forth. "Keep us posted, Miss Molly."

"I will."

"Have a fun morning!" Amelia said.

"You too! Hope you find nice scarves!"

I found Mom and Daddy in a cozy little sitting room on the other side of the front door. It was just as Christmas-y in there as the rest of the house. Mom had a fluffy white blanket on her lap with puffballs all around the edge that would probably make a cat go cuckoo. The two of them were reading and drinking coffee—only doing two things at a time instead of Mom's usual seventeen. I was glad for both of them that they got to be resting. But after a while, that kind of quiet sitting stuff kind of makes me want to run around like crazy.

"Once Wally and Amelia are back from shopping, let's go do that too," Mom said to Daddy (too bad for him). "What are you up to, Mol?"

"Watching Teddy and Pip. But I wanted to see you guys first." I gave her a hug and then hugged Daddy, too. "I'll see you later. Enjoy the charm and shops. Then later, you and me—outside. Right, Daddy?"

He smiled and nodded.

That was going to be the best part of the day for me (after hanging out with Teddy and Pip). Depending on what kind of snow we had going on, Daddy and I would make a snowman or go sledding.

"Molly Jane, we do not like that thing. We try to be not complaining so very much for our Amelia who sewed it up for this very trip and likes it a whole lot, but we do not prefer it."

"NO GOOD! WE ARE SQUISHY SQUISHED IN THAT THING! WE ARE NOT BABIES—WE ARE JET EYES WHO SOLVE CRIMES AND WRITE HIT SINGLES! BEW BEW! BAILIFF, TAKE IT AWAY!"

"I promise you won't be in this for very long," I said. "We're only going up to that bedroom I'm staying in. It will take a few minutes and that's all. That's shorter than one of Pip's songs, I bet."

"PIP'S SONGS ARE GOOD LONG ROCKING SONGS, MOLLY JANE! THEY ARE MORE TIME THAN STAIRS! THEY ARE LONG LONG LONG!"

"Okay. But the time for being in the carrier and going up the stairs will be short. That's the point. We need to get upstairs because the bedroom I am taking you to is where we start the hunt for clues."

"CLUES, SHOES, BLUES, NEWS! PIP IS A ROCK STAR, NOT A SMALL BABY! HERE COMES A HIT SINGLE!"

Pip is not a baby.
Pip rocks and rocks and ROCKS!!
Pip is not a baby in a crib!
Pip is not a baby.
Pip does not cry.
Pip is a dude.
Pip is a tough guy!

Baby sacks are not for a dude like Pip,
And maybe they are not for Teddy, too.
Or either.
Pip is a tough guy who does not ever cry,
and baby sacks are the worst of times!
No good!!
The end.

"THE SONG WILL BE LONGER AND LONGER, TOO. I AM ONLY STARTING ON THIS THING, MOLLY JANE. OKAY? OKAY."

Amelia was sure right about them not liking the cute guinea-carrier. I had to use some parent-talk to get them to let me put them in it. Like, saying we would have to stay downstairs and they would have to be in the small travel cage if they didn't let me take them upstairs. Stuff like that. I couldn't even believe I was talking like that, but I felt like I had no choice about it. Tucking them into that thing was the safest way to get Teddy and Pip from down here to up there in this big old house with so many stairs to climb. I mean, what if I dropped one of them? I did a shudder when I thought about that. Plus, I had to carry the litter box, too.

So it was not easy or quiet, but I finally got them in the carrier's pockets. "It'll only be a minute—I promise!" I said, talking louder than their complaining so they could hear me.

Then they switched to guinea pig sounds and got even louder.

"Wheek wheek wheek! Whoop whoop whoop!"

"WHEEEEEEEEEK!   WHEEEEEEEEEEEK! WHOOP WHOOP WHOOP WHOOP WHOOP!"

"Here we go!" I walked nice and slowly up the winding staircase to Elizabeth's room. It was kind of a funny and tickly time, actually, with the two of them squirming against my stomach in the carrier.

"Molly Jane, are we done yet? I do not enjoy this thing or this walking up and up and up the stairs. Or being so very close and squished with that Pip."

"WORST OF TIMES! PIP IS NOT A HAPPY DUDE! I FIRE THIS THING AND THE STAIRS AND STAIRS AND—THE END! PIP IS WHO IS SQUISHED, NOT TEDDY! PIP DOES NOT DO ANYTHING WRONG! PIP SAVES THE DAYS!"

"Hang on, guys. We're almost there!"

"ALMOST IS NOT THE SAME AS BEING ALL DONE WITH THIS SQUISHY-SQUASHY THING! 'ALMOST' IS NOT THE WORD THAT PIP WANTS TO HEAR RIGHT NOW!"

"Pip, you are not making things easy on Molly Jane. Maybe you can keep it zipped?"

It was like that every step of the whole way. Believe me, it was a big relief to set their litter box in the doorway to Elizabeth's bedroom and then get those two out of that carrier. "Whew!"

"YES, WHEW!" Pip copied me. *"WHEW WHEW AND BEW BEW!"*

"Thank you, Molly Jane, for no more of that thing!" Teddy scratched behind one ear and then the other. Then he started up an all-out bath. *"Teddy does not prefer that thing, Molly Jane. Please, for me, tell Amelia. We love our Amelia, but not the thing. Okay? Okay!"*

"SQUISHY SQUISH SQUISH SQUISH SQUASH SQUASH!" Pip went on and on as he paced back and forth by the bed. *"THE END! THE END!"*

"Okay, okay. We're all done with that," I said. "All finished. And now you can walk around as much as you want and stretch out," I said.

"STRETCH STRETCH, FETCH FETCH—WE ARE NOT BARK-BARKING DOGS OR BABIES, EITHER!"

"So this is Elizabeth's room."

"But this is Molly Jane's room," Teddy said. *"There is no person called Elizabeth in this very house, unless she is a ghost or monster."*

"No, she isn't a ghost or a monster. She is a real person, a grown-up, who used to live here. She lives somewhere else now. When she lived here, this was her room. For now, it is my room."

Teddy scratched some more. Then he said, *"Okay."*

"MOLLY JANE, WHAT ARE YOU SAYING?! IS THIS PERSON A PERSON OR A GHOST OR A MONSTER?"

"Person. For sure. Don't get freaked out."

"PIP IS NOT FREAKED OUT!"

"Anyway, this room is where we are going to start our mystery!"

"Oooh! Molly Jane has a twinkling Christmas tree all of her very own in this room!" Teddy cooed quietly.

"Yep!"

"Many twinkling trees are here in this big haunted house, not only just one like at our perfect house with a walkway. Our Wally and Amelia, too, have a twinkle tree in the room where they do their sleeping, here in this haunted house. But sadly, there is no tree twinkling in the room where Pip and me do our sleeping. Not even one tree. No tree at all. No twinkling. Uh uh. No tree for Pip. Or me."

I sat on the floor and pet Teddy's soft little head for a while. "I'm sorry, buddy. Maybe I can find one for you and move it to your sleeping room. What do you think?"

"Teddy thinks that would be good. Thank you, Molly Jane. I will wait for you to now do that thing. Except maybe I do not want to be alone so very long or much in this room with only Pip to save me from

ghosts and monsters, so please do not leave me. Thank you. You can find Teddy's very own twinkle tree when our best friends Wally and Amelia are back. Thank you!"

"Okay—but Teddy, sweetie, this house is totally safe, totally not haunted."

"IT IS HAUNTED! DO NOT SAY IT IS NOT! DO NOT SAY TEDDY AND PIP ARE CRAZY!"

"Molly Jane, it surely is haunted. I am sure of it. Pip and me know when a house is that thing. But we are safer here because all best friends are together here—except for not Max. And also our Wally did not make any monsters mad exactly here with his hammering and sawing. I don't think. It is not his fault that monsters are here, so we are safe. I think. So far."

"EXCEPT MOM JANE IS HERE! DO NOT FORGET THAT THING!"

"But—"

"AND ALSO NOW THE ROCK STAR WOULD LIKE A TREAT! THANK YOU, MOLLY JANE! PIP IS NOT AFRAID TO STAY HERE WHILE YOU GET THAT THING. TEDDY, DO NOT BE A BABY!"

"Do not say that thing! Teddy is surely not afraid of . . . things! Very much."

"Pip, you just had a treat right before we came up here," I said. "I know you did, so don't try to trick me."

"TRICKS AND TRICKS AND STICKS AND BRICKS! MOLLY JANE, I AM WANTING A TREAT! THIS IS NOT A JOKE!"

Pip is me—and a treat will be

The way to solve a mys-ter-y!
Pip is me—and "no treat" means we
Won't catch a bad guy—NO-SIR-EE!

"Nice one, Pip."

"*THE HITS ARE NOW COMING TO ME. THAT HIT I JUST DID FOR YOU IS CALLED 'PIP WANTS A TREAT.'*"

"*Pip, you are forgetting to have manners,*" Teddy said. "*Molly Jane is a best friend, not a person who only brings treats to you when you want that. We love Molly Jane and do not want her to leave us alone in this room in this very haunted house.*"

"*PIP LOVES MOLLY JANE, YES, BUT ALSO AND TOO VERY MUCH WANTS A TREAT! THANK YOU! DID YOU HEAR THOSE MANNERS?*"

"*That is better, but still not so good.*"

Pip is me—and a treat will be
The way to solve a mys-ter-y!
Pip is me—and "no treat" means we
Won't catch a bad guy—NO-SIR-EE!

"I know! Let's look for clues," I suggested. "Then, in a while, we can have a treat."

"*CLUES, SHOES, BLUES, NEWS!*" Pip yelled, while Teddy yawned a very cute guinea pig yawn.

And then Pip started chewing on the green rug.

"Let's not do that, okay?" I said about the rug.

"*ONLY PIP IS DOING THIS, MOLLY JANE, NOT OTHERS. AND PIP IS BORED NOW AND WANTS TO CHEW THAT THING VERY MUCH. IT IS VERY CHEWY! CHEWY CHEW CHEW! BEW*

BEW! I KNOW!! AFTER THE TREAT, WE WILL
PLAY VADER! MOLLY JANE WILL BE VADER, AND
WE WILL CHASE YOU!"

"Looking for clues is very exciting!"

"TREAT TREAT TREAT TREAT!"

"Treat treat treat treat!" Teddy surprised me
by joining in.

"You guys!" I laughed. "Seriously? Is this how
it's gonna be?"

*"Yes, Molly Jane, this is how it is and will be.
We are seriously wanting treats, both Pip and me. I
have decided that thing to be a 'yes.' Tee hee! But I
am asking please and thank you in a polite way. And,
too, I am saying that I love you, Molly Jane!"*

"TREAT TREAT TREAT TREAT!"

"Well, okay, but that means we have to get all
packed up in that carrier again to go downstairs," I
said. I really hoped that fact would get them to change
their stubborn little minds. "I really can't leave you
alone in here. We need to stick together."

*"Molly Jane, we are not so very far, I don't
think, from the room that is our safe sleeping place in
this haunted house. That place, too, is up and up the
stairs and stairs, so we think it is near. And we do
not need to ride in the carrying thing to go to that
place. I do not think. Pip and me can walk with our
feet and would prefer it. Thank you."*

*"YES, LET US GO TO OUR VERY SLEEPING
PLACE FOR JUST A TIME, AND YOU, MOLLY
JANE, CAN RUN RUN RUN DOWN THOSE MANY
STAIR STEPS AND GET US A TREAT IN A BIG BIG
HURRY! OKAY? OKAY! THE END! LET'S GO!"*

"Go, Molly Jane, go!" Teddy giggled. *"And also, please find a twinkle tree for Teddy's sleeping room now. Thank you! Or sooner!"*

Those two totally know how to wrap their adorable fuzzy selves around my thumb or finger or heart or wherever. I would go downstairs and find them a treat, of course, and they knew it. And also, if I had any hope of getting going on a mystery even a little bit, I had to do it fast.

The hallway between Mom and Daddy's suite and Wally and Amelia's was not very wide, but it was pretty long and had some turns to it. I let Teddy and Pip run, staying close to the wall, for as long as they wanted to—but that wasn't for very long. Then I had to pick them both up and carry them. And for some reason, they started making loud guinea pig noises while we walked.

"Wheeeeeeeeek! Wheeeeeeeeek! Wheeeeeeeeek! Wheek wheek wheek wheek wheek wheek wheek!"

"WHOOP WHOOP WHOOP WEEEEEEEEEEEEoooooooooooWEEEEEEEEEEEEEEooo oooooooooo!"

"Here we are," I puffed. "Wally and Amelia's suite." Teddy and Pip's room in the suite was pretty small and was almost like a porch on a house, except upstairs and inside. Okay, so it wasn't like a porch. Maybe it was another sitting room. Yeah, that's more like it. There was an old-fashioned couch in there and also a bookshelf, plus the guys' nighttime travel cage on top of a card table. Fancy glass doors separated the sitting room from Wally and Amelia's bedroom in Suite One. "Safe and sound. There you go."

They started up some loud wheeking again when they saw the cage, their water, and hay. It was like they couldn't even help it because they were so excited. When I set them down, they both ran to get a drink of water, squealing and wheeking away.

"Wheeeeeeeeek! Wheeeeeeeeek! Wheeeeeeeeek! Wheek wheek wheek wheek wheek wheek wheek!"

"WHOOP WHOOP WHOOP WEEEEEEEEEEEEooooooooooWEEEEEEEEEEEEooo ooooooooo!"

"I didn't know you were thirsty!" I called over the noise. "Why didn't you just tell me?"

"What's going on?" Daddy was suddenly right next to me, which gave me a startle. "I heard the ruckus and thought you might need help."

"Yeah, well, maybe I kinda do," I said.

"DAD DAN! DUDE! YOU ARE HERE!" Pip had water dripping off of his chin when he yelled.

"Dad Dan?" Teddy said more politely. *"You are having a truly good day of it, here in this haunted house? Yes?"*

Daddy did a chuckle and rubbed at his nose. "I am having a fine day. Thanks for asking."

"You are welcome for the asking."

"How're your allergies?" I asked.

Daddy smiled and said, "I'm fine, sweetheart."

"WE ARE DONE WITH POLITE NOW, RIGHT? MOLLY JANE NEEDS TO RUN TO GET TREATS FOR HER FRIENDS! SEE YOU LATER, MOLLY JANE! RUN RUN RUN!"

"Pip, try to have a manner," Teddy sighed. *"We do not get to see this Dad so very much, and so we should be friendly when we do."*

"Um, would you mind . . ." I looked hard at Daddy's nose to see if it was runny, ". . . watching these guys while I run downstairs to get them a treat?"

Daddy shrugged and said, "I guess I could do that." He had a thick book in his hand whose title sounded like a mystery.

"Don't read that to them," I said quietly.

Daddy looked at his book. "Oh. No, of course not."

"GO, MOLLY JANE, GO!"

"Do not forget Teddy's tree!"

"I might have to do that later," I said. "I can't get back real fast with treats if I have to look all over for a tree, too."

"Okay, Molly Jane. You can do what you can do and that is all. Dad Dan, will you tell us jokes? We would like that very much more than just sitting together with no jokes," Teddy said.

"YES YES! TELL US A JOKE! MAKE IT A GOOD ONE!"

"You want jokes, huh?"

"BUT NO TRICKS! AND WE WANT THE JOKES TO BE FUNNY, DADDY-O!"

Daddy looked at me.

I shrugged and wished him good luck. "I'm going now," I said.

"GOODBYE, MOLLY JANE! DO NOT FORGET ALL ABOUT US AND OUR WANTING TREATS!"

"Thank you, Molly Jane!"

I noticed a closet in that sitting room whose door was not all the way closed up. The detective in me needed to take a peek before I left. Even though I was under a bunch of pressure to get going.

"Which of Santa's reindeer has bad manners?" Daddy asked the guys.

"DAD DAN, DUDE! DO NOT SPEAK TO US OF REINDEERS! REINDEERS EAT GUINEA PIGS! EEK EEK! WORST OF TIMES!"

"Do a different joke that does not scare us out of our little heads, okay, Dad?"

"*Rude*-olf," Daddy said. "Get it?"

"No, I do not get it. Do a different joke. Please."

"WHAT ARE YOU SAYING, DADDY-O?! DO NOT TELL JOKES ABOUT REINDEER, WHO EAT GUINEA PIGS, OKAY?"

I smiled and shook my head. "You guys are silly," I said over my shoulder.

In the little closet was a bunch of stuff for little kids, like toys and baby chairs and stuff. Perfect! I dug through a box and found a couple things for Teddy and Pip. I left them out for later.

Probably the best thing I found in that closet was a red plastic wagon. It seemed like just the right size for pulling guinea pigs down a long hallway between two bedrooms. The sides were high enough for safety and it was easy to pull (I tried it out). Great! We could totally use it when I got back. I got a towel out of the bathroom closet and put that in the wagon.

"DAD, YOU ARE BEING A SILLY!" Pip giggled.

"Oh, am I?" Daddy laughed.

"Silly sil sil! Tee hee!" Teddy agreed. *"It is much fun to have a talk with Dad Dan while we wait for treats. Molly Jane? Are the treats coming? Today?"*

Chapter Eight
Maybe a Clue . . . ?

It took longer than I expected to get back with a baggie of washed and dried lettuce, celery, carrots, and broccoli—even with Mom's help. And after all that, I found my dad, Teddy, and Pip all totally napping. I am not even kidding about that.

Usually, when there is food around, the guinea pigs do a huge bunch of wheeking, whooping, and begging for treats. I mean, they beg for treats even when there aren't any treats around. But when they smell something, look out.

This time they were totally silent, totally still and zonked out in their Christmas sleeping bags with only their cute faces peeking out.

I might've been a little upset about it, but they were so cute that I really couldn't be. I bet you couldn't have been either.

I gave Daddy a poke on his shoulder, but he stayed sleeping too. Good grief.

Well, I needed to do something with my time while those boys napped, right? But what? I set the baggie of veggies on the window sill where it would stay cool. Then I thought about what to do next. I needed the guys for exploring Elizabeth's spooky closet, so that would for sure have to wait. I did want to check out that playroom in the tower, though, and I couldn't see an easy way to do that with Teddy and Pip along. Maybe this was my chance to see it by myself—even though I would've liked to have my dad go with me. Maybe it was best to let him have his nap and watch the guys, save his energy for snow-time later. I needed to be brave and go alone.

I will admit to you readers that I was a little bit creeped out by this idea, even though it was my own. I have a good imagination and imagined lots of creepy things as I made my way up the narrow and winding stairs. I guess all the talk about haunted houses wasn't helping much. I mean, it's not like I was walking up to or into the Nubb house at Halloween, or something worse than that. It was just a staircase leading to a tower room that was an old playroom full of cool sparkly stuff. Probably.

At the top of all those stairs was a closed-up plain wood door that I expected to be locked tight. Did I hope it was? Maybe.

But it wasn't. When I tried the knob, the door opened right up for me.

"Okay, here you go," I said out loud to myself. "A sparkly princess playroom, that's all." I calmed down my imagination and stepped in.

"Or . . . not." Instead of finding a magical princess playroom tower with sparkly stuff all over the place, I found a pretty boring storage room. "Rats." There were labeled brown boxes all over the place, and lots of them said "Christmas." The only interesting things, actually, were the oval-shaped windows on each wall, decorated with those colorful Christmas lights I had seen from the car when we drove up yesterday.

I imagined the place as a playroom back when Amelia was a kid, and I liked what I imagined. Too bad it hadn't stayed that way.

As long as I was up there, I poked around in some opened-up boxes and was lucky enough to find a perfect little plug-in Christmas tree for Teddy. For some reason, nobody wanted to use that one for decorating, but I thought it was perfect. I knew Teddy and Pip would love it, so I put it by the door.

After that, I got busy reading labels on other boxes like a detective would do. I mean, I might as well look for anything about *P* or *O*, right?

But nothing at all jumped out at me, except I did see a spider. And then I had to work real hard not to freak out and run all the way down those stairs to get Daddy to take care of it for me.

I calmed down and found my bravery again. Then I moved far away from that spot.

So far, the tower room was turning out to be just like the basement of our house—except that it was upstairs. So it was actually like an attic instead, but with cool windows. Not a place full of toys or sparkles or clues.

I was about to give up when I kind of accidentally knocked over a stack of empty Christmas decoration boxes. Oops. And under all that stuff was a dusty old box labeled "Danby." And my detective senses started tingling away!

I picked up the box, which was a little dusty and gross on the outside. It wasn't super light, but it was also not too heavy for me to lift. I didn't open it. I put it next to the little tree by the door. I wasn't too sure if opening it would be invading privacy or not. I would bring it downstairs and ask Wally and Amelia for their opinions about that.

When I saw the spider again, I picked up the little tree and the dusty old box and left the tower attic room real fast—after closing the door behind me, of course.

When I got back to them, Teddy and Pip were awake and wheeking up a storm for their treats.

"Wheeeeeeeeek! Wheeeeeeeeek! Wheeeeeeeeek! Wheek wheek wheek wheek wheek wheek wheek!"

"WHOOP WHOOP WHOOP WEEEEEEEEEEooooooooooWEEEEEEEEEEEEEEooo ooooooooo!"

The noise made Daddy slowly wake up and looked confused about where in the world he even was.

"How did you guys all end up asleep?" I wanted to know.

Teddy stopped wheeking and squealed. *"Oooh! Molly Jane brings a twinkle tree! Thank you, best friend! Where did you find this thing for Teddy?"*

"MAKE IT TWINKLE, MOLLY JANE! DO IT, DO IT, DO IT!"

Daddy stood up and stretched. Then he kissed the top of my head. "What's this, then?"

I explained where I got it from and why. "I hope nobody minds that I brought it out of the tower room," I said.

Daddy took the tree from me and looked it over for dangers. "Looks okay to me," he said. Then he plugged it into an outlet and set it on the floor. He looked it over again and sniffed it and whatever. "I think that'll work just fine. But I'll ask Rosalie to be sure." Daddy yawned and mumbled, "So sleepy," and then yawned again real big. "I'd better find Mom. See you later, kiddo. Guys."

"ORRIE VWAH, DADDY-O!"

"Goodbye, best friend Dad! Thank you for trying hard with the jokes!"

"MOLLY JANE? WHERE WERE YOU BEING INSTEAD OF HERE WITH YOUR BEST FRIENDS AND WHERE EVEN ARE OUR TREATS?!"

"We thank you very much for the twinkling tree, but we are very hungry!"

"Yeah, well, you two totally fell asleep, so I went exploring."

"YOU DID THAT THING WITHOUT ALL BEST FRIENDS TOGETHER?!"

"You were sleeping," I said again. "So yeah, I did, all by myself. And now we are going to explore together."

"After we eat treats."

"WHERE ARE THE TREATS, MOLLY JANE FISHER?!"

"I am going to make a game out of finding those treats," I decided on the spot. I set the old Danby box down by their travel cage and brushed off my jeans and shirt a little bit.

"Molly Jane, do not put us in a box, please. Or a bucket. Or anyplace. Thank you. Pip and me do not

*like to be put . . . in things. For times. You know that
thing!"*

"NO GOOD! DON'T DO IT!"

"This box isn't for you. I promise. But I do have
a different and better idea for getting you guys back to
my room. It's not the carrier and it's not walking. Are
you ready?"

They let me know that they weren't actually
one bit ready and wanted their treats there and now. I
ignored that and picked up Teddy. I put him right in
that wagon without any explaining. And also without
giving him time to argue about it. I put Pip in real
quick too. It worked like a charm. I think they were
too surprised to get all upset about things.

I grabbed the baggie of treats from the window
sill and started down the hallway.

When I heard Pip say *"WHEEEE!"* and Teddy
said, *"Wheeee for Teddy, too!"* I knew they liked the
wagon just fine—which was a big relief. Finally,
something was going right.

The idea that came into my brain was a game
that mixed up exploring and eating veggies. I decided
to call it "Hide and Treat."

I left them in the wagon in the hallway while I
zoomed into the room and quickly hid the veggie
treats all around—in places they could get to pretty
easily. I didn't want the game to be frustrating for
them.

*"Molly Jane?! Why is it that we are in this
wheely wheel wagon and you are in there doing
sneaky things without us?"* Teddy called.

"DO NOT SNEAK OR BE A SNEAK, MOLLY JANE! DO NOT EAT OUR TREATS! WHAT ARE YOU DOING IN THERE?!"

"One more minute!" I called back. I had one more carrot to hide and was standing in front of Elizabeth's closet, trying to decide. I had a tingly detective feeling about it, you know? I needed to explore it real carefully, because there was just something about it. I knew there was.

But I needed Teddy and Pip in there with me. I mean, if they didn't find anything to worry about, it was for sure safe. And I needed to give them a good reason to go in there. I gave the carrot a toss and heard it hit a wall. "Okay, guys—I'm all done!"

Chapter Nine
Hide and Treat

Finding treats in a
Haunted house bedroom
Sneaky sneaking round and round.
Molly Jane hides them,
Pip and Teddy find them—
Best and worst of times all in one!
CRUNCH!

Finding treats in a
Haunted house bedroom
Sneaky sneaking round and round.
Lettuce (YUM!), broccoli (YUM!)
And carrots, too (YUM YUM)!
Best and worst of times all in one!
CRUNCH!

It didn't take very long for the guys to find the hidden treats and eat them up. I mean, it *really* didn't take long. Maybe it took five whole minutes and that's all. Guinea pigs have real good noses for treats, and they like to eat them more than just about anything.

I was happy that they ate every scrap so there was nothing to clean up . . . or to have to ask Mom to clean up. Or whatever.

"One more!" I said when, just like me, Teddy and Pip had saved that closet for last.

"Molly Jane, I know there is a treat in that place, but it is dark and scary and probably there are monsters in there too. I am asking, please, if you will go get the treat for us so Pip and me do not have to be scared out of our heads but can also have the treat. Which we like and want very much. Thank you."

"GO, MOLLY JANE, GO!" Pip squeaked. *"MONSTERS WILL NOT EAT YOU, MOLLY JANE. I AM PRETTY SURE OF IT."*

I have to admit that my fingers and toes were tingling because I didn't want to go in there either. "How about if I shine a flashlight?" I asked.

"NOPE! GO!"

"I do not think that will help. Monsters are not afraid of flashlight lights and will still probably eat us anyway."

"What if I tell you that my dad went in there yesterday and said it's totally safe and fine?"

"Dad Dan is a best friend, and we do believe in his words. Except he is a big man and we are small guinea pigs. Monsters can eat us—we know it. Dad is not monster food, but we maybe are. And also, mostly, if Dad says it is fine, then why does Molly Jane not believe in him and go in there by her very self?"

Good point.

I hadn't noticed because I was watching Teddy, but Pip was suddenly standing very still in the doorway of the closet. *"NO SOUNDS. BUT . . . NO GOOD,"* he whispered. *"TOO TOO QUIET. THE MONSTERS ARE MAYBE SLEEPING IN THERE. THEY WILL SURELY WAKE UP SOON AND START CLICKING. AND THEN THEY WILL EAT US. PROBABLY. WORST OF TIMES."*

"Sorry, Molly Jane, but I am thinking that maybe, possibly, Dad Dan is not right about this place being safe or okay for us guinea pigs."

"Let's try the light," I said. "And we'll go together." I shined the flashlight in, but it didn't help much. They didn't like the way the light made shadows on the walls (and maybe neither did I). "Well, what are we going to do? You guys still have one more treat. Are we going to leave it in there?"

"Molly Jane? Please please please?" Teddy begged.

"MOLLY JANE, MONSTERS WILL NOT CRUNCH YOU. I AM NOW SURE OF IT. YOU WILL BE OKAY. GO GET IT!"

I took a deep breath. "Okay. Fine." I was being totally cuckoo for being so nervous. There was nothing to be afraid of in a closet that Daddy had checked over only a half day ago. "You're right. There's nothing to be afraid of."

I started to walk slowly toward the turn inside the closet with the flashlight shining on only empty walls so far.

But then I noticed that the guys were right behind me. Then they were in front of me. Then they forgot to be freaked out. That carrot was so close that they started wheeking and whooping and ran real fast ahead of me.

After only a couple of seconds, Teddy ran past me and right out of the closet with the carrot in his mouth.

"NO FAIR! NO GOOD! MOLLY JANE, TELL THAT DUDE THAT THIS IS NO FAIR!"

"Crazy Pip! Teddy was the bravest one who got the treat, and so he is the one who gets to crunch it most of all!"

"Guys?" I interrupted their arguing, "Did you see anything else in there? I mean, like a clue or anything that might be a mystery? Or anything?"

"NOPE." Pip ran over to Teddy so he could take a bite of the carrot.

"Only this treat," Teddy said with a little shrug—then he took his bite out of the other end of the carrot.

"Really?" For some reason, I just couldn't leave it alone. I felt my detective senses tingling and telling me that there was something in there. I had to know what clue was in that crazy, deep, winding closet! Why was it so hard to go in there? It didn't make any sense. I needed to be braver.

I worked up my courage all over again, because this time, I was going in. I took a step. Another step. One more step farther into the closet. . . .

"MOLLY JANE! STOP! DO NOT DO THAT THING YOU ARE DOING! DO NOT GO! PIP WILL DO IT! PIP WILL SAVE YOUR DAY!"

"No, Teddy will do it! Teddy loves Molly Jane and will save her day, not this crazy Pip!"

"PIP LOVES MOLLY JANE AND WILL SAVE HER DAY! DO NOT SAY HE WON'T OR THINK YOU WILL DO THE SAVING INSTEAD!"

"Um . . . ?" This time, the guys actually raced each other right around me. What a couple of little knights in shiny armor, huh? "Thanks, guys!" I called after them. Then I shined the flashlight for them and waited.

"Oh! Oh! Molly Jane, there is a thing!" Teddy called back. *"You were right about that stuff! There is a something in this very place!"*

"There is?! What kind of a thing?"

"DO NOT LISTEN TO THAT DUDE OR ASK OF HIM WHAT IT IS! PIP FOUND IT! IT IS PIP WHO FOUND THIS THING WHICH IS MAIL!"

"Teddy found it!"

"IT IS NOT POSTCARD MAIL, BUT REGULAR MAIL—AND PIP FOUND IT, NOT TEDDY!"

"It's mail?" I asked. "Like a letter?" Whoa! This was a big deal. No, this was a *huge* deal! How could mail at the back of a deep dark closet *not* be a clue?!

The letter got dragged out by one guinea pig and then the other until they got to where I was standing and dropped it.

"Thank you so much!" I said to both of them. I pet them equally, both at the same exact time, until they purred like crazy. Then we all left the closet and those two argued even more about who had saved the day for me.

"You two are knights in shiny armor," I said. "You're heroes!"

"Yes. We are heroes. Thank you, Molly Jane, for knowing that thing. Bad Barbara steals the mail and hides it in that place in this haunted house. That is called the mystery, right?"

"BAD BARBARA IS HERE IN THIS HOUSE! PIP KNEW THAT THING! EEK EEK! SHE STEALS THE MAIL AND HIDES IT, AND THIS IS THE WORST OF TIMES!"

"Guys, this is for sure not about Barbara. Don't freak out! You two are heroes. Let's think about that."

"ROCK STAR AND HERO IN SHINY ARMOR IS PIP! PIP PIP HOORAY! I WILL WRITE A SINGLE ABOUT THAT STUFF, BUT MAYBE NOT RIGHT NOW."

"Well, let's see what this is, okay?"

"OKAY!"

"Okay, Molly Jane! Let us now see what letter Bad Barbara steals and hides!"

What it was, was an old, old, old letter addressed to Elizabeth Danby. That was not so super surprising, since this was her closet. But you know what *was* super surprising? The old, old, old letter was sent to her by Evelyn (Evie) Dearling.

Chapter Ten
The Letter

Besides the fact that it was written by the person who was Scary Evelyn now (probably back in her teenager years), the weirdest thing was that the letter never got opened. After years and years, it was still sealed with a sticker on the back (a gold circle with the letter *D* on it). Why wasn't it opened? Did Elizabeth decide she didn't like Evelyn after all and not even want to open her letter? Did she throw the letter in the way back of her closet and leave it there for a zillion years? I mean, I might not be a fan of Amelia's grown-up sister, but that seemed pretty mean. Especially if Elizabeth was supposed to be a friend.

And also, if Elizabeth did decide she didn't like Evelyn anymore, why not throw the letter away? The not-opened letter at the back of the closet seemed very fishy. I thought about it and thought it about some more, but only ended up stuck.

The Danby family moved away right after Amelia's family visited Christmas Castle for the last time. That was right after Elizabeth and Evelyn turned into best friends. Maybe the family moving away was a clue.

I sat on the bed and wondered who I could go to so I could ask a bunch of questions about this stuff. I mean, who could I ask without getting in trouble for disturbing peace and privacy?

"*WHAT ARE YOU DOING, MOLLY JANE FISHER?!*" Pip was looking up at me from the green rug. "*WE ARE HERE AND YOU ARE HERE AND SO WE ARE HERE. TOGETHER. AND WE ARE BORED NOW AND WANT TO DO THE THING OF SOMETHING! OR ELSE MORE TREATS WOULD BE OKAY.*"

"*Molly Jane, can Teddy come up on that bed that looks like a covered-up wagon? It looks some fun.*"

"Um . . ." I gave myself a little shake to change the subject in my brain. "Sorry, guys—I was thinking about . . . how about a wagon ride?"

"*Molly Jane, do you mean the very bed you sit on is a pretend wagon, or are you saying to us that we will ride in the wheely wagon from before? Days ago or months or weeks . . .*"

"The wheely wagon from before," I said. "That'll be more fun than being on Elizabeth's bed."

"*WAGON IS OKAY. LET'S GO. WAGON IS DOING SOMETHING.*"

"*Okay, Molly Jane. Teddy, too, will do the wagon!*"

While I slowly pulled Teddy and Pip (and the litter box) up and down the hallway, I did some big thinking about mysteries that were possibly popping up. Was the old dusty Danby box a mystery or a clue in a mystery? What about Evelyn's letter? Neither thing seemed one bit like the kind of mystery I was expecting: an old box and an old letter.

And I couldn't open either thing without getting in some trouble, which was frustrating.

Also, until I talked to Nora, I wouldn't know if the mystery was even about *P* and *O* anymore.

"WHEEEE! WHEEEE! WHEEEE!"

"Wheeee! Wagon ride is fun! Go, Molly Jane, go! Tee hee!"

I stopped pulling. "Oh! I just remembered!"

"What, Molly Jane? What is it that you remember? Teddy would like more wagon time, thank you. Let us do more and more of it. Tell us the remember-y and then pull pull pull! Wheeee!"

"GO, MOLLY JANE, GO!"

I pulled some more: back to Elizabeth's room, turn around, back toward Suite One. "There are fun toys I want you two to check out."

"Did you say the word of 'toys' to us?"

"TOYS?! BUT WE ARE NOT BABIES! MOLLY JANE, DO NOT MAKE US MAD! DO NOT PUT US IN CARRIER!"

"I meant machines, not toys. Music-making machines and . . . um—here." I stopped the wagon in their sleeping room. I lifted Teddy first and then Pip and set them in the travel cage.

"Well, here you go, Pip! A music machine!" I set the colorful toy xylophone in the cage and waited for Pip to finish guzzling water and then check it out.

"MUSIC MACHINE? FOR PIP?" he whispered. He snuck closer and closer, just like he did when he

was checking out Mom's cell phone last year. *"MUSIC MACHINE?"* He sniffed at it before backing away again. *"THERE IS NO MUSIC. WHAT IS THIS THING?"* he whispered. *"COLORS AND COLORS AND SHAPES AND . . . WHAT ARE YOU DOING, MOLLY JANE?! NO NO—!"*

I gave the middle yellow bar a tap with the little plastic hammer.

Ping!

"OOOOH!"

Pong!

"I SEE AND I HEAR! THIS THING IS FOR PROBABLY HIT SINGLES!" Pip inched closer again. *"IS THAT WHAT IS TRUE, MOLLY JANE FISHER? THIS THING IS FOR MUSIC-MAKING? FOR ROCK STARS LIKE PIP?"*

"Exactly," I said. "I made the sound with this little hammer, but I bet you could make smaller sounds with your toenails."

"SMALLER SOUNDS SOUND NO GOOD. PIP WILL MAKE BIG SOUNDS."

"Okay." I handed him the little plastic hammer. "Try this, like I just did. Can you hold it in your mouth?"

"PIP CAN DO IT," he whispered, and then he picked it up.

"Or you can just use your feet," I said again, because it looked like it would be a lot of work to play a xylophone with a little hammer in your mouth.

After he set the hammer down and said, *"PIP CAN DO IT!"* he picked it up again. He got it in the right place, with the hitting part close to his mouth, and then climbed right up on the xylophone.

Ping, pong, ding, ding, tink, tink, TINK TINK!

"Good *job*, Pip!" I laughed. "Awesome!"

Pip pinged or dinged every musical rectangle. Then he dropped the hammer and said, *"BEST OF TIMES! TEE HEE! THE ROCK STAR IS LIKING THIS MUSIC MACHINE! MAYBE IT IS BEST OF TIMES!"*

"Molly Jane, please, for your friend Teddy, say now that this music machine will go away some of the times while we are staying in this haunted house. Please? Teddy will not like to hear that thing day and day and night and night for days and months . . ."

Ping, pong, ding, ding, tink, tink, TINK TINK!

"Don't worry, sweetie. Wally and Amelia will be in charge of how much of the time it stays in there with you guys."

"Maybe Teddy will not need to hear this music machine all the time and all the time again. Again and again and again—"

"Do you want to see the machine I picked just for you?"

Teddy was adorable with the little-kid light-up learning game I brought for him. He pressed on the square when it lit up and then the game said the color, or the picture on the square.

"Blue!"

"Chicken!"

"Circle!"

Teddy thought it was very funny.

"But Teddy does not need to learn this stuff, Molly Jane. He knows his colors and shapes and chickens very much already."

"I know. This is just for funny fun."

Ping, pong, ding, ding, tink, tink, TINK TINK TINK TINK TINK TINK!!

"Oh my goodness!" Amelia laughed as she came in. She scooped up Pip. "How wonderful, Pippen! Listen to you! And my darling Teddy, aren't you the most amazing love ever!"

"Amelia, my friend, it is not called amazing. It is only banging and bonging, and it is the same for both machines, except Teddy makes words come out of his machine."

"But it *is* amazing!" Amelia said again. "Where did you find these things?" she asked me.

When I showed her the closet, she wanted to look through all the toys too. I explained about the wagon while she did that. "They really, *really* didn't like the carrier," I said.

"Oh, I'm sorry, Molly. I shouldn't have insisted . . . oh look! You boys have a tree of your own now, too!" Amelia smiled and shook her head. "Thanks to Molly?"

"I found it in the tower room," I said, which made her look surprised at me. "Daddy said he'd ask Rosalie if it was okay to bring it in here. But he checked it out first and it seemed safe and fine to him."

"It seems fine to me, too," she said. "How very thoughtful of both of you! Thank you!"

"You're welcome."

"Dan did say something to me just now about the tree being okay with Rosalie. Now I know what he was talking about."

Wally scooped up Teddy and cuddled him while he agreed about his talents with the lights and words game.

"*Yes, Molly Jane finds a twinkle tree, a wagon, and also the learning machines to keep your best friends busy,*" Teddy said, and then he licked Wally's hand. "*Pip is banging, binging, and bonging on that music machine, Wally. He does that for much time and now is done with that. I think. I hope. I am asking. We, too, had a game of Hide and Treat and found mail in Molly Jane's scary closet full of monsters.*"

"Did you say mail?" Wally sounded real surprised.

"*Yes. Mail. Bad Barbara hides it there, just like the postcards were hiding that one time not so long ago, or maybe long ago.*"

"But Barbara—?"

"*PIP DID IT! PIP SAVED THE DAY! PIP STOPPED BAD BARBARA FROM DOING . . . BAD THINGS! AMELIA, PIP WOULD LIKE TO NOW DO MORE ROCKING. THANK YOU!*"

Amelia set Pip down by the xylophone. "You found mail in the tower room?" she asked me.

"Not in the tower room—in my closet. I mean in Elizabeth's closet," I said. "But I did find a box in the tower room that said 'Danby' on it."

Amelia's eyes got wider about that.

"It's over there," I pointed.

Wally was still holding onto Teddy (whose little eyes were shut real tight as the xylophone got going again). He walked to the box and had a look.

Ping, pong, ding, ding, tink, tink . . .

"Well, well, *well*," Wally said. "Interesting."

"I thought it might be." I held out the letter to Amelia and she sucked in her breath. Her eyes got big too. "Oh my goodness," she said again.

"Oh my goodness, too," Teddy said. *"That thing was far far back in the scary dark closet full of monsters and possibly Bad Barbara did it. Teddy found it and brought it out for Molly Jane."*

Wally and Amelia looked at each other. "And the boys were in the closet because . . . ?" Amelia sounded confused.

"We were playing a game," I said, suddenly feeling like maybe I shouldn't have let the guys go in the closet after all.

"There was a crunch-crunch carrot in the very back of that place," Teddy shared. *"It was roly and poly and good for crunching. Teddy got it out, for Molly Jane, to save the day. And also there was that mail. Teddy was a hero. Or was a night."*

Ping, pong, ding, ding, tink, tink, TINK TINK TINK TINK PING!! "DO NOT FORGET, FRIENDS, THAT PIP SAVED THE DAY!"

"Pippen, my dear fellow," Wally said. "Good job on whatever part you played. And now, let us go downstairs for a while. I believe you need a rest from your music-making."

"NO NO! THE HIT SINGLES NEED TO COME OUT, WALLY! THE FANS WANT HITS!"

"I have set the travel cage by the front window, so you two can watch the world go by for a while."

"PIP DOES NOT WANT TO WATCH THAT THING! PIP IS A ROCK STAR, NOT A WORLD-WATCHER! PIP NEEDS TO ROCK!"

"Wally, I am happy to do anything except hear Pip's music some more. Thank you," Teddy said.

Chapter Eleven
Sneaky Peeking

"NO GOOD! NOT FUN! THERE IS NOTHING TO WATCH OUT THIS WINDOW! IT IS ONLY SNOW AND SNOW AND SNOW!" Pip complained.

"But there is something to watch, Pip! Surely there is! Look look! There is a human, right there, walking back and forthly in front of this very house in the snowy snow. See? See? Look at her walking walking walking walking . . ."

Wally and Amelia were in chairs in front of the fireplace, ignoring Pip's complaining one hundred percent. (I don't know how they can do that!)

"EEEK! PEEKING! WALLY! AMELIA! MOLLY JANE! WALLY! AMELIA! THAT GIRL IS PEEKING AT US THROUGH THIS WINDOW! HELP! HELP!"

That had to be the caretaker's daughter, right? The girl with the tight-crossed arms? There could hardly be anyone else out here in this woodsy, snowy place.

"Eeek from me, too!" Teddy agreed. "Surely this human is a sneaky spy! Soon she will call the government and they will come with lab coats for Pip and me! Look look! Help help!"

What if she *was* spying? And what if she found out the secret?! I was worried too. I know how people can see and hear things if they are looking and listening enough. I also know what a huge mess it can turn into if the wrong person finds out the secret. It can be a mess even if I only *think* someone knows the secret.

Wally knows that too, but this time he only said real calm sentences. "Guinea pig sounds only, boys, until she stops looking. It's alright. Don't give her anything to see but your dashing good looks."

Teddy and Pip started up some loud but regular guinea pig wheeking and whooping. I guess that was all that was going to happen about the peeking girl.

I kept worrying and thinking stuff like, what if that girl had super good hearing? What if she had seen their little mouths moving like people's do? What if she already saw them making words? Kids notice stuff like that, especially kids who love animals. I hoped that girl didn't actually love animals. Which was a super weird thing for me to think—believe me. I didn't really wish that. I just wished she hadn't peeked in at Teddy and Pip!

"So what about that box?" Wally said.

"Oh yeah, the box. Well, I was thinking, since it's been sitting up there for *so* long that it got dusty, maybe nobody would care too much if we, you know, looked in there," I said with a little shrug. I was trying to do what Daddy calls "playing it cool."

Wally said, "I see."

"It's not like we would invade privacy. We wouldn't open any sealed-up stuff. Or anything like that. We'd just open up the *box*."

Amelia said, "Uh huh."

"It's been a long time since those people even lived here, right? Like longer than I've even been *alive*."

Amelia laughed a little about that and sipped her tea.

And that's when I figured out that maybe I had said something about her being old without meaning to. Oops! I sure didn't mean to do that, and I didn't think it either.

"You are not wrong, Molly. It would have been twenty-five years ago that I last visited this house. That *is* a long time. And the Danbys moved away shortly after that visit. And they did leave this box behind."

Wally (who is real quick and smooth with stuff like smoothing out feelings) did a little smile and said, "It is impossible to believe that you are older than twenty-five, my darling."

Amelia smiled back at him, shook her head a little, and sipped her tea again. Then she looked down at her phone. "Oh! I have just gotten a text back from"—she lowered her voice real low—"Evelyn."

"Oh?" Wally's eyebrows went up. "Isn't she in London, darling?"

"Indeed she is, but she has her phone in front of her as ever, apparently," Amelia sighed. "She says to go ahead and throw the long-lost letter away. Or, if I am curious, I may open it for my own sake and curiosity."

Wally said, "Really?" in a surprised voice.

"Naturally, she is laughing it all off as unimportant," Amelia sighed. "Or so it would seem."

Wally said, "Naturally," with a little sigh too.

"But I truly believe that it may be *very* important," Amelia said. "It should have been important to her to know that the letter was never opened. For her to know that maybe Elizabeth did not abandon her as a friend. What if it was all a big misunderstanding? You and I know all about that, don't we, my dear?"

"Indeed we do."

"GONE NOW! GONE! HELLO? FRIENDS? THE SNEAKY PEEKING HUMAN GIRL IS NOW GONE FROM THIS WINDOW. PIP IS TELLING YOU THIS NEWS! ARE YOU HEARING THIS NEWS?"

"Pip is right. The girl has gone away and is not looking or peeking anymore. If you humans are now done talking about mail, Teddy would like attention. Okay? Okay! Thank you!"

My parents and their phones were off at the shops, but I needed to call Nora. I asked to use Amelia's phone, and she very nicely said yes.

I got in the right spot for less crackles and asked, "Did you call Max?"

"Hi, Molly," she said. "Nice to talk to you, too."

"Sorry. Hi, Nora! How are you?"

"Fine."

I waited a few seconds. ". . . That's it?"

"Yeah. I guess."

"Oh, okay. So I'm super excited to hear about your talk with Max! Can you hear me okay?"

"It's not too bad. A little crackly."

I moved closer to the window. "Better?"

"Yeah. Stay right there."

I could see Jess in the driveway of the little house, kicking snow with her boots. "Well? Did you call Max?"

"Yes. It was scary to, but I called your cousin. You owe me one, Molly Fisher."

"I know. You told me that before you did it. Thank you, thank you, thank you!! What did he say? Is Tweets alright? Has he done more Morse code letters?"

"Max said . . ." Nora did a long pause that went on and on (just to drive me cuckoo).

"Are you still there? Don't be mysterious. Tell me!"

"Max said Tweets is totally fine."

"Whew!"

"He let him fly around and everything yesterday."

"He *let* him, huh? I bet the real story is Tweets totally escaped on him."

"He did more Morse code, yes, but . . ." Nora paused again for a zillion years.

"Nora! But *what*?!"

"But he only did *P* and *O*."

"Oh," I said in a big gushy breath. "Well, okay."

"Max also said to tell you to remember that he is a dude who takes naps and watches TV and stuff. This is Christmas vacation and so he is not always listening to your bird's beak-tapping."

"That sounds exactly like Max." I did a big sigh. "Okay. Thanks. It's a disappointment, but I am real grateful to you for asking."

"You're welcome. What's new there?"

"I found a letter!"

"You found a letter?"

I told her all about Hide and Treat, ending the story with the guinea pigs running out of the closet with that old letter.

"Who was it from and to?"

"From Amelia's sister to Elizabeth—who used to have the bedroom I am sleeping in now. She was the owners' daughter."

"Do I know about Amelia's sister?"

"It's Scary Evelyn," I said real quiet. Wally, Amelia, and the guys were back in the kitchen, but I really didn't want to take a chance of being heard by them. "Remember what I told you last year at Christmas?"

"But what was *her* mail doing in the closet at your vacation house?"

"It was there for, like, twenty-five years!" I explained about the Dearling family spending vacations here. Then I told the story of how Evelyn and Elizabeth were friends when they were teenagers. "Then the Danbys sold this house and moved away, without even letting their friends know about it. They didn't tell Evelyn where to send mail or anything! That sounds fishy, right?"

"Very fishy," Nora agreed. "Maybe . . ." She did another long pause like she does.

"Maybe what?"

"Maybe somebody in that family didn't like Evelyn being friends with Elizabeth. Maybe they hid the letter so she wouldn't write back. So those girls would stop being friends."

"Whoa." I thought about that for a while. And even though it was real tricky to not agree with Nora's ideas, the truth was, this one didn't make sense. If a person wanted to break up Elizabeth and Evelyn's friendship, why not throw the letter away or burn it up? Why would a person leave it in a closet where it could be found one day and wreck the plan?

But I kept the thoughts in my head and said, "I think you are onto something, Nora," instead.

After that, we talked about Peanut and Coco and what Benny Nubb was up to in Westerfield, until the front door opened and Mom and Daddy came in.

Oops! I had just talked on Amelia's phone for a half hour!

Chapter Twelve
Fun in the Snow

"Ta-da!" It was one of our best snowmen ever. Daddy and I finished up with two not-quite-matching stick arms and a carrot from the fridge (don't tell Teddy and Pip that part).

If you haven't tried making one with a tiny amount of snow, or the wrong kind, you will really have to trust me on this: it is much easier to make a snowman when there is a lot of good snow on the ground. Daddy and I really have tried all kinds.

We did a high five and a hug—and then he started up a surprise snowball fight with me. My dad doesn't do snowball fights like, for example, a fifth-grade boy. He doesn't throw hard or ever aim at my face. He aims at my middle instead or down at my feet. He throws so the snowball hardly even hits me and doesn't care if I *do* throw my hardest—and aim wherever I can. I really appreciate that and really appreciate my dad. He is the best.

I stopped the battle and told him that.

"Love you too, kiddo," he smiled.

So anyway, it was fun to make snowballs and hide from Daddy and try to hit him, even though I never did.

I was hiding behind the big blue house with a really good snowball, all ready for another try, when I saw that girl again: Jess Ellington.

She crossed her arms up at me, just like Nora does when she's good and mad, and then she stomped away to her little house. I hadn't done a single thing to deserve that, so I felt a little upset at her.

And I was so distracted that Daddy totally snuck up on me. He got me with a snowball, too. "Ha *ha!*" he said as the snowy thing splatted on my back. "Gotcha!"

"You sure did!" I laughed, and then I threw my snowball and actually got him . . . on the elbow . . . a little bit.

"And now you got me back," he said.

"Sort of. A little," I said.

Daddy said he had to get inside to clean up a bit before dinner. "You coming too, Mol?"

"I think I'll stay out here a little while longer." Only because I wanted to peek in that front window to see what that girl could have seen when she was peeking in at Teddy and Pip.

"Okay. Have fun." Daddy turned back when he was a few feet away and said, "Maybe you'll get a chance to make a new friend."

He said that because he saw that girl outside by her house again, with her arms still crossed up super tight. Daddy has a lot of faith in me as far as uncrossing tight arms, I guess. Maybe—probably—too much.

Well, now that I knew Jess was outside, I couldn't really check out the front window like I wanted to. Since I couldn't do that, I really only wanted to go inside to find out what Amelia had read in her sister's old letter.

But something inside of me said I really should try to be nice to that girl. Plus, Daddy and Amelia had faith in me about that and thought it was a good idea. Maybe I should try.

I walked real slowly through the deep snow. I was in no hurry at all to talk to her. I had to watch my feet so I wouldn't fall, but when I looked up, there she was. Her arms were crossing tighter and tighter at me until I was a little bit worried she would get stuck that way forever.

"You can't come over here," she said in a quiet but not friendly voice. "This is called private property."

I stopped walking. "Okay," I said with a shrug.

"You have to stay over that line." She pointed down at a line I could tell she just drew in the snow with a stick. "And I have to stay over here."

"Fine." So I stayed on my side and she stayed on hers with her arms crossed or frozen tight. So far, this was pretty dumb. "I'm Molly," I finally said. "What's your name?"

She didn't say anything for a while, and then she said, "Jess."

So I said, "Hi," again.

"Hi."

We stood there for a while, not saying anything else. "Why can't you come over here?" I asked.

"I don't know. I mean, it's my house."

I felt my eyebrows go up.

"Sort of," she mumbled. "It used to be." She shrugged again. "Mom said I can't."

That was a good enough reason for me. We just stood there in the snow up to our knees after that, not talking one bit, which was not very comfortable.

"If you want, we could play," I said, even though I didn't really want to.

"But I can't go in there," she said, sounding mad. "And you can't go in my house either. Those are the *rules*. And I have to stay behind this line."

I guessed she was in trouble with her mom for peeking in the window before. "Well, then we could write letters to each other. I do that with my friend Nora. Sometimes."

She didn't answer right away, so I thought she was thinking about it (she wasn't). "My grandma's dog steals letters."

That was a very weird and confusing change of the subject, I thought. I stared at her for a while then said, "Really?" I wasn't sure if I should smile or not because I didn't want to make her mad again.

But when she (almost) smiled at me, I let my face copy. "I don't know why he does it. He just does it," she said. "Sometimes. I mean, he used to."

My right-away thought was that (oh no!) maybe Fluffy had died too. And that was way too much sad stuff for one kid to deal with all in one swoop.

So I was real relieved when she said, "He lives in the little house now. With us."

"Oh."

She pointed at the big blue house with her mitten. "I lived there with my parents and Grandma and Fluffy. Before."

"Oh."

"Me and Mom and Fluffy were there for Christmas, too—before you guys came."

I wondered if she wanted me to be sorry for being at Christmas Castle. It didn't seem very fair of her to think like that, though. Wally rented the house. It was a business thing. That's what the big house was *for*.

But then I remembered all of that sad stuff she had going on in her life and gave her a break.

She didn't seem like she wanted to say more about that subject anyway, so I asked, "Where did Fluffy put the mail he stole?"

"Different places," she shrugged.

"Can you give me an example?" I giggled. "I am very curious."

I was real amazed to see a grin on her face when she said, "One time, we found the electrical bill behind the *toilet*."

I couldn't help laughing about that and was glad to see she was laughing (a little bit) too. "At least it wasn't *in* the toilet!"

She nodded. "Lots of times, we found stuff in his bed, like, under his toys. That's his favorite place to put letters."

"So do you check Fluffy's bed, like, every day, just in case he stole your mail?"

She nodded.

"Like, checking the mail means checking Fluffy's bed, too?"

She nodded some more.

"What kind of a dog is he? A retriever?"

"Poodle."

"Oh. What color?"

"White."

"Well, I love animals, so could I meet him?"

She shrugged. "But he doesn't go outside, except to—you know."

"Well, if I see him outside, I'll come out, okay?"

"Okay."

"My parakeet's name is Tweets, and he can do Morse code."

"Does he talk?"

"He says 'pretty' and 'hello' and 'hello pretty.'"

She smiled. "What color?"

"Green and yellow."

"You have guinea pigs, too. I saw them in the window." Her smile went away after she told me that. She was probably remembering the trouble she was in.

"Those are my friends' guinea pigs. Their names are Teddy and Pip."

"I love guinea pigs," she said quietly.

"Me too. I wish I could have one, but my dad is allergic to animal fur."

We stood there in the snow for another while. She shoved her hands in her pockets real deep. "I saw you making a snowman with your dad."

I shrugged and then said, "Um . . . yep."

After a long time of not talking, she said, "My daddy is doing work in a place far away."

"How come?"

She shrugged. "He's an engineer, and sometimes he has to go to far places to help people. Places without phones, even."

"Like, he works with trains?"

She looked at me for a while like I was cuckoo and then shook her head. "He tells people how to build things real safe and strong. Like buildings and bridges."

"Oh."

"He is helping in a place that had lots of stuff and buildings wrecked by a huge storm. There's hardly any electrical stuff left."

"That's nice of him."

She shrugged.

"But I'm sorry for you," I said, and I actually meant that. "You must miss him a lot."

She nodded down at her feet.

"I'm sure he misses you a lot, too—like a ton."

She shrugged again, and then mumbled, "Not very much, I don't think."

"Of course he does!"

"But he didn't send a single thing for Christmas." Jess kept looking down at her feet.

Wow, that was so sad I could hardly even stand it! No wonder she was in a bad mood and jealous about me and my dad. I had no idea what to say to her about any of that. "Well, I hope you hear from him soon. I'm sure you will. Real sure."

She didn't say anything back.

"Um, I should go inside now. My toes are getting numb. I'm from New Jersey where it's a lot warmer and muddier than here."

She nodded down at her feet a little bit. Then she turned and walked away toward the little house.

Chapter Thirteen
Advice and a Bubble Bath

The clawfoot tub Mom was so thrilled about seemed a little slippery to me. But I guess I liked it otherwise. I liked how it got totally full of bubbles, like, right up to my neck. That was awesome!

My toes were all thawed out now, and I was safe and warm. I felt so lucky, sitting there in the bubbles, knowing my mom and dad were right there in that house with me. And Tweets was fine and getting some flying time. And also my favorite people and guinea pigs were downstairs, too.

"Mom?"

Mom peeked in the door right away. "Whassup?"

I told her all about meeting Jess and about her sad times that were going on.

Mom's face got full of sympathy, and then she said, "Oh, that poor dear."

"Yeah. I didn't want to meet her one bit, but now that I did, I really wish I knew how to help her."

Mom came in and sat on the closed-up toilet seat. "I think you helped her already, Molly—by talking with her this afternoon."

"Maybe. I guess. But I wish I could do more than that. Talking doesn't make her exact problems better. Not for real."

She smiled at me. Then she said, "Know what?"

"What?"

"You're a good kid, Molly Jane Fisher." I blew some soapy suds at her off of my hand, and she said, "Most of the time," and laughed, wiping the suds off of her face.

I sank back into the tub until only my face was out. Then I sat up real sudden. When I did that, I kind of sloshed soapy water onto the floor a little bit (or maybe a lot). "Oh my *gosh!*"

"What? What just happened?" Mom asked.

"Nothing happened—sorry to scare you. I just got an idea!"

Mom shook her head at me. Even though she was still smiling, she sighed and got a towel to soak up the puddle I had just made on the floor. "Well? What's the big idea?"

"Jess's grandma's dog steals mail!"

Mom stopped cleaning and stared at me.

"Her grandma's dog is a poodle named Fluffy. He steals mail," I said.

"O . . . kay?"

"What if he stole something important—like a Christmas letter from her *dad*?!"

Mom sat back on her heels. I could tell her brain was working hard. "Um . . ."

I sucked in my breath. "Mom, what if Fluffy stole Evelyn's letter too and hid it in Elizabeth's closet?!" I was getting excited and kinda splashed soapy water out of the tub again.

Without even stopping her big thoughts, Mom wiped up more water. She had a confused frown on her face—I suppose because I had not told her the whole story about Evelyn's letter.

So I explained that part. ". . . and it was never even *opened*, Mom. The dog probably took it and hid it so Elizabeth never even saw it. That poodle wrecked her friendship!"

"Um . . ."

"Evelyn totally thought Elizabeth was being mean and wasn't her friend anymore. But Elizabeth thought the opposite, so she didn't write to Evelyn, I don't think. Then she even moved away from here without telling Evelyn a new address."

Mom shook her head a little bit to catch up with the story.

"But the truth was that Elizabeth didn't even open Evelyn's letter. Mom, those teenager girls stopped being best friends for no good reason! Because of a poodle!"

Mom nodded, but then she shook her head in a not-good way for my mystery. "Sweetheart, that letter would have been sent over twenty years ago. Maybe more."

"Twenty-five," I said.

"Well, sorry, babe, but I don't think your mail-stealing poodle could've even been around way back then. Dogs don't live that long."

"Oh," I sighed. "Rats."

"It *is* an interesting theory," she said as she handed me a dry towel. "And it is possible that the dog could've stolen something more recent. Look, I think it's almost dinner time. I'll get you some PJs, and then we'll comb through that crazy hair."

"But, wait! I know!!"

Mom got startled all over again when I said that (kind of loud). "Now what?" she laughed with her hand over her heart.

"I can share my grandmas with her!"

"You can—? With—?" Mom shook her head again to catch up with me.

"With Jess. Sorry, I didn't finish the thought."

"Oh," she eventually said with a little smile. "You can share your grandma club with Jess. Sweetheart, that is a lovely idea."

"I am so lucky to have so many—and those grandmas love to get letters and to send them, and so, why not? Everyone wins!"

Mom nodded and smiled.

"We could give the grandmas envelopes with Jess's address already on them and make it super easy for them. Would you help me with addresses and stamps?"

"Of course." Mom smiled at me some more, shaking her head (this time in a good way). "Yes. Tell you what, kiddo: I will also jot down the address of Shady Acres for Jess. You can list all of your adopted grandmas' names and let her pick one." Mom must've seen my face kind of fall, because then she added, "Or maybe she could just write to them all."

"That sounds better."

Chapter Fourteen
Teenager Evelyn

Okay, so it probably wasn't Fluffy the poodle who stole and hid Evelyn's letter. He wouldn't have even been born yet twenty-five years ago, like Mom said. But she was right: he sure could've stolen something *else* important, like some mail that came from Jess's dad less than a week ago.

Jess said she and her mom were living in this house right before Christmas. I'm sure they were super busy getting things ready for us back then. If her mom is anything like mine, she has seventeen things going on at all the same time, all the time, and especially right before Christmas. My point is, she could've set a stack of mail down one day, gotten distracted, and then—Fluffy.

The more I thought about it, the more excited I got, because there could totally be an important letter from her dad in this very house, waiting for Jess and her mom to open it! Anything can happen when life gets cuckoo like that, right? And lots of stuff can happen when your pets are amazing.

While Wally chatted with Rosalie (who was setting up our fancy dinner), Amelia and I shared a chair by the fire and read Evelyn's letter to Elizabeth (from twenty-five years ago, not a zillion).

Amelia says people wrote a lot more letters twenty-five years ago than they do now. There was no email or texting back then. Can you imagine that? Calling on the phone was kind of expensive, too, so parents wanted their kids to write instead. Stamps were, like, less than a dime. Amazing stuff. Amelia used to love to write and get letters.

Anyway, this is what Evelyn's old letter said:

Hi Liz,

I promised to write first, and here goes. I want to thank you so much for listening to all my troubles when I was at your house. Sorry to have been such a downer. It was really good to know that someone understands about things like that, about how it hurts to lose someone you thought really cared about you. Mom keeps saying I was too young to have a boyfriend anyway and my dad says he wasn't good enough for me. That doesn't actually help. But you understand. I am getting over him by listening to my favorite songs on my record player and I got a new haircut and some new shoes. I feel so lucky to have a new best friend to share all of this with. Well, I better end this so I can get it in the mail and off to you as soon as possible. I can't wait to hear back from you, Liz! And I will talk my dad into coming back to the house a lot sooner than Christmas!

Bye for now!

BFFE&E&E&E&E&E!

Evie

When I finished reading, I looked up and saw tears in Amelia's eyes.

"Oh dear," she sighed.

"Stolen mail sure causes trouble for your family," I said.

She nodded while she folded up the letter.

"Your sister thought her new best-friend-forever totally dumped her—just like her boyfriend did."

"Yes. I think so, Molly. It's very sad."

I thought about what it would be like if Nora stopped talking to me, or moved away and didn't tell me where she went to. Except Nora and I have been friends since we were born, practically—and she lives across the street. And also, her mom would for sure tell my mom if they were moving.

I imagined it with Penny for a better example and decided it would hurt a lot.

But what if Elizabeth Danby felt the exact same way Evelyn did? Maybe she felt like *her* new best-friend-forever didn't even write to her, and *that* hurt a lot. Maybe she didn't bother to try to find Evelyn because of that. Maybe it was a mixed-up communicating problem.

It felt like the postcard mystery all over again, only different and an older mystery that no one was asking me to solve right now.

Okay, it was different—but it *was* about mail getting lost and how that wrecks friendships.

But how in the world did that letter end up in Elizabeth's closet if it wasn't Fluffy who stole it? That was a fishy puzzle and too much of a coincidence.

In case you don't know, coincidence is when two things happen that are really alike, but are not relatives. Or something like that.

"The things that shape us," Amelia was saying. "Oh, poor Evie."

I actually had to agree with her about that, which was another miracle. Sorry for Scary Evelyn is the last thing I ever expected to feel. "Maybe we can help them get back together," I suggested. "Maybe if your sister knows that Elizabeth never got her letter, she'd feel different about her. Maybe they could be friends again."

The dinner bell tinkled from the kitchen, and Amelia tucked the letter into her sweater pocket. "Maybe," she said, but the way she said it told me she didn't have much hope.

The table was set for us like it was Christmas all over again. This time, the food was meatballs and mashed potatoes, vegetables and bread. Even though I usually would rather have pizza or pasta, tonight I liked Rosalie's choices just fine.

It helped a ton that we had chocolate cake for dessert, served on Santa Claus plates with a plop of whipped cream. The whipped cream had red and green sugar sprinkles on top, too. (Mmmm!)

When I brought up the great idea about searching for Fluffy's stolen mail, every grown-up stopped eating and stared at me.

"Jess's dad must've sent a card or a letter, but she didn't get it—or anything—from him on Christmas!" I explained more. "I am so sure Fluffy stole it and hid it in the house somewhere. *So* sure." I took a bite of my cake while I waited for someone to agree with me.

"It *is* sad," Mom finally said—and everyone else nodded. "And it's possible that the dog did do something with it. I will keep my eyes open. I promise."

"Me too," Amelia said.

"And I," Wally nodded at me.

I looked at Daddy, and he looked back. "Well, yeah. Sure, kiddo. If I see anything, I'll let you know ASAP."

"You guys are awesome," I said.

"Molly? Wally and I are planning a stroll around the property tomorrow morning—if it isn't too cold," Amelia said. "Could you—?"

"Watch Teddy and Pip while you guys walk? Yes!"

"And Molly Jane, do not forget Teddy. Your hero night will keep his eyes open for more lost mail—unless he is sleeping. I have already found mail in this haunted house today, so I know I can do it another time too."

"EXCEPT IT WAS PIP WHO FOUND THAT MAIL. DO NOT FORGET THAT IT WAS PIP WHO SAVED THE DAY!"

"No no! Teddy is the one who—"

"Is there any chance there's more stuff in the back of Elizabeth's closet?" I interrupted.

The guys stopped arguing and both shook their heads real fast. I think the truth was that they really didn't want to look in there again.

"How about if I check it out?" Daddy offered real quietly.

"Thanks, Daddy. Look behind the toilets, everyone," I said, which made them all stop eating again. "Fluffy puts things in places like that. Jess told me."

"Well, I would imagine," Mom said, "that Rosalie would have discovered something hidden behind a *toilet* by now. She does an amazing job of keeping this place up."

"Yeah. I suppose you're right," I slumped.

"But it would only take a second to double-check," she agreed. "Which I will."

I could hardly even wait to start the search for Jess and Rosalie's letter—even though it still had nothing to do with *P* or *O*. What in the world was Tweets' Morse code message about?

"Rosalie has agreed to open the Danby box," Wally suddenly said, which was a big surprise I couldn't believe he had saved for dessert. "And she has promised to let me know if anything comes out of it that will interest us. Especially something that would give us a clue about where the Danby family went when they left here."

Chapter Fifteen
Guinea Pig Charades

Have you ever played charades? It's really fun, but also goofy because you can't talk but you need to get your team to guess what book or movie or song you are acting out. Playing charades with talking guinea pigs is a whole different deal. This is how that went. . . .

Teddy and Pip can't read or write, you know, but they were on a team with me and Daddy. Mom, Amelia, and Wally were the other team. We agreed to only pick movies, songs, and books that a fourth-grader and Teddy and Pip could know about. I knew that didn't give the grown-ups a lot to work with, but if we didn't do it like that, Daddy would have to do all the work, and also, probably, the other team would totally win.

It was such a happy cozy time, sitting by the fire and that beautiful Christmas tree. Snow was falling outside again, music played quietly in the background, and I felt like the luckiest person anywhere ever. And then I felt sorry for Jess all over again.

"*Molly Jane? You are not paying attention! Watch what Dad Dan is doing!*"

"*YOU ARE NOT BEING ON THE TEAM AND MAKING US WIN WIN WIN!*" Pip squeaked at me. "*WHAT IS DADDY-O DOING? IS HE BEING A SILLY OR DOING A CLUE?*"

Daddy was making the motion for "movie." Then he tapped on his arm twice. That means "two words." He held up a finger.

"FINGER!" Pip yelled. "*PIP SOLVES THE PROBLEM! IT IS FINGER!*"

"*Pip, Dad is telling us about a movie, not about a piece of his person. Stay quiet. He is not done so far.*"

Daddy smiled and shook his head. Then he started pointing up at the ceiling.

"*No? Is it 'no'? No, it is not 'no'?*"

"It's not 'no,'" I said helpfully.

"*Is it upstairs you are saying to us, Dad? Up stairs and stairs and stairs is our sleeping place. And our twinkle tree! Is the movie about a twinkling tree, Dad?*"

"*WE DO NOT LIKE THE BABY CARRIER!*"

"Ceiling?" I guessed.

Daddy shook his head. Then he walked to the window and pointed again. He pointed and pointed.

"*SNOW! PIP GOT IT! PIP SAVED US ALL! IT IS THE WORD OF 'SNOW'!*"

"Snow White?" I guessed, but Daddy shook his head and then tapped on his lip.

"MOUTH?"

"*Dad, are you saying it is Snow Mouth?*"

Daddy started laughing and shook his head.

"SNOW LAUGHING? SNOW MOUTH LAUGHING? SILLY SILLY DADDY-O SNOW MOUTH LAUGHING? NO MOUTH? SCARY! NO MOUTH IS SCARY!"

"Pip, those things are not a movie that we ever knew of! Do not be a silly!"

"BUT DADDY-O IS GIVING THOSE CLUES AND SO I AM GUESSING AND GUESSING! DO NOT SAY I AM DOING IT WRONG! PIP IS SAVING THE DAY AGAIN!"

Daddy waved his hands in front of him in a crisscross. I told the guys that that means "never mind and start over."

He went to the window again and pointed out and up. Then he made his fingers wiggly and pointed again.

I frowned, but then I took a guess and said, "Stars?"

Daddy got real excited and nodded a lot.

"YES? THE MOVIE IS CALLED 'YES,' DADDY-O?"

"The first word of the movie is 'stars.'" I said. "Right, Daddy?"

Daddy nodded.

"Yay!" I started bouncing in my seat. "Got that, guys?"

"OVER AND OVER, MOLLY JANE!"

"Teddy has it!"

Daddy held up a finger.

"The first word is stars," I said again.

He shook his head. Then he changed his mind and nodded.

I felt confused and stopped bouncing.

"Dad is being silly again!"

"DADDY-O, WHAT ARE YOU SAYING?! ARE
YOU TALKING ABOUT STARS FOR A MOVIE OR
NOT STARS?!"

Daddy went to the window again and did the
same pointing and wiggling fingers, and then he held
up one finger.

"Oh my gosh, I know!"

"PIP KNOWS! PIP SAVES THE DAY! 'DADDY-
O IS A SILLY'—THAT IS THE ANSWER!"

"Pip, that is still not a movie we know of. You
are the one who is silly."

"One star?" I guessed. "Not stars, just star? I
know what it is! I know what it is!"

"Molly Jane, what in the world is it?!"

"DO NOT SAY IT! DO NOT SAY IT! PIP WILL
DO IT! PIP KNOWS HOW TO DO IT!"

I covered my mouth with both hands so I
wouldn't say it out loud. I had to let the guys try to
figure it out, but it was so hard!

Daddy was making shooting motions with his
hands that made my mom look like she wished he
wasn't doing that.

"NO GOOD! DANGER! BAD GUYS! WORST
OF TIMES! BEW BEW! BEW BEW!"

"Dad, are you showing us a bad guy? We do
not prefer that. Show us something else."

"Maybe, yeah," I said, after I uncovered my
mouth. "Maybe get them to guess it a different way."

Daddy stood there thinking for a while, then he
did a really funny clip-clop trot around the living
room, like he was riding a horse. It made everyone
laugh, like, a lot. It was very silly.

"TEE HEE!"

"Tee hee hee! Dad, that is some funny! Tee hee!"

Daddy kept clip-clopping, and we all waited for Teddy or Pip to get it.

"Dad, are you playing cowboys now? Are you riding on a . . . horse?"

Daddy nodded and nodded and pointed at Teddy.

"Not bad manners, right? The word you are doing now is horse?" Teddy guessed.

"STAR HORSE?!" Pip yelled. "IS THAT THE ANSWER, DADDY-O? THE MOVIE OF 'STAR HORSE'? I DO NOT KNOW THAT MOVIE, BUT I AM SAVING THE DAY FOR OUR TEAM BY SAYING THAT STUFF!"

Daddy made circles with his hand and then pulled on his ear. I explained that that means it sounds like "horse."

It took a while and lots of guesses of other words that rhymed with horse, but they finally got it.

"VADER!! WORST OF TIMES IS THAT GUY! I BLAST THAT GUY WITH MY BLASTER! BEW BEW!"

"Good job, Dad! You did a good turn and the answer to it all is the movie of Star Wars! Do we win the game, Molly Jane? Do we get a prize or a treat or both things?"

When charades was done, Mom went upstairs to have a soak of her own in that claw-tub. Daddy sat in the sitting room with his mystery book, and the rest of us sat by the fire and the Christmas tree. Wally read a book out loud to Teddy and Pip. He must've done a lot of looking to find a story they had no objections about, didn't scare them, and that they didn't feel like they needed to stop every two words. I had never read the story or even heard of it. It was really good.

Amelia held Teddy in her lap and I got Pip. It was so sweet and nice, holding that little guy and petting him and knowing he was calm and listening to the story without any worries in his amazing mind.

When the story was done, Wally and Amelia each carried a guinea pig up the staircase (walking real slow and not using the carrier). "Good night, Molly!" they called.

"Good night, best friend!"

"GOOD NIGHT AND SLEEP TIGHT! PIP DOES NOT KNOW WHAT THAT MEANS, BUT DO IT, OKAY, MOLLY JANE?! DO NOT SLEEP LOOSE, OKAY?"

"Okay!" What a good day. I felt comfortable and sleepy and like I could go right to bed too—except I still needed to call Nora.

I did more yawning during our talk than Nora appreciated. "Maybe you should call in the morning when you have more energy for me," she said.

"Sorry! I'm more sleepy than tired, if you know what I mean. Anyway!" I shook myself to wake up a little better. "So yeah, I *am* coming up with clues and mysteries now, but still nothing about Tweets' letters. Any ideas, partner?"

"*P* and *O*," Nora said. Then she said it again a few more times. "*P* and *O*. *P* and *O*. PO. PO—Molly? What if Tweets is talking about the *post office*?!"

Chapter Sixteen
Christmas Castle

During another huge breakfast, Wally told the story that Rosalie had told him about the house we were in. I tried hard to keep my mind on that mystery, but the rest of my brain was buzzing and spinning about Nora's genius clue about the post office. *P* and *O*: post office. Did that mean Jess and her mom's missing letter from her dad was still at the post office? Tweets somehow knew—I have no idea in the whole world how he can do that—that there was missing mail, and he told me with his beak that it had something to do with a post office . . . three hours away . . . that he never saw in his whole life. Wow.

Anyway, the story of the blue house is a long one with lots of details, so I will give you a shorter version of it. Wally is great, but sometimes he really is a professor about things. I will give you the facts of the matter and you can decide if it is important for finding or solving a mystery.

1. First, the house was owned by the Danby family. Like, they had it from when it got built. They lived here for almost 100 years!

2. When the Danby family's children moved out and got their own houses, the house was too big for only the parents, so they turned it into a B&B.

3. Eventually, the youngest boy, who was Elizabeth's dad, ended up being the owner.

4. But Elizabeth's dad didn't really want to do that for his job. He had other ideas and plans that he was working on. He did not tell his kid about those plans.

5. An opportunity came up all of a sudden back in the year when Amelia and her family visited that last time. Mr. Danby was working hard on selling the house and getting ready to move during that very visit.

6. The house got sold to the Ellingtons.

7. As soon as the Dearlings left from their vacation, moving trucks came and loaded up stuff, including Elizabeth's stuff. Except for that letter from Evelyn.

8. The Ellingtons were kind of rushing the Danbys out of the house, like they couldn't wait to be the owners and start the business up.

9. The Ellingtons were Rosalie's husband's parents.

10. All this stuff happened before Rosalie knew any of them, but she knows the story because her husband's mother told her.

11. Mrs. Ellington thinks the Danbys did not leave their new address with the new owners because they didn't want to be

bothered about any problems. They only left the name of their lawyer.

12. Because there was no address, that meant that anything they forgot had to stay with the Ellingtons.

"You learned a lot," I said, shaking my head at Wally. "You could make a good detective when you want to stop being a professor."

Wally chuckled at me. "Rosalie is quite willing to chat while she works," he said. "All I did was listen. She also left a note for me this morning when she left this lovely breakfast."

Amelia said, "Oh?"

"Yes, darling. She has already gone through the box that Molly found in the tower room and has found something that she would like to show us."

I know you guys are dying to know what it was, so I won't make you wait (like I had to). So Rosalie came over to the house to clean up our breakfast like she did the other days, too. Mom was already doing the cleaning up, of course. Rosalie gave her a little talk about how Mom was the guest and this was Rosalie's job, so Mom should relax instead of working. (Rosalie doesn't know my mom, so I will give her a break about that way of thinking.) Anyway, she had a letter (yep—another one!) in her pocket and handed it to Amelia as soon as my mom sat down and relaxed.

Do you have a good guess about the letter? Well, it was a twenty-five-year-old letter from Elizabeth Danby to Evelyn Dearling.

This letter had no stamp and no address, either. It only had Evelyn's name on it. The return address was the blue house we were sitting in with our mouths hanging open. It sure looked to me like Elizabeth was waiting for her friend Evelyn to write first so she could have that address to write down. And that is definitely not the same thing as not wanting to be friends ever again.

But she never got it, did she?

Why not? Because the letter ended up way back in her deep closet. That part was still a big weird mystery. None of us could figure out why in the world the letter from Elizabeth got put in a cardboard box, either, or why it ended up in the tower room, where it sat and sat for twenty-five years.

Missing mail. Two missing letters. Maybe Tweets meant more than just the missing Christmas letter when he tapped his *P* and *O*.

We would have to wait for Amelia to check with Evelyn again before we opened the old letter from Elizabeth. It was good manners to do that— to give the ladies their privacy—even though Amelia was about ninety-five percent sure her sister would say she didn't care and we could open it or even throw it away.

Chapter Seventeen
Jess Ellington

I had two mysteries to solve and both were about mail. P and O was most probably for "post office." Wow. But our time at Christmas Castle was ticking away on me. How in the world was I supposed to get it all figured out by tomorrow morning when we had to leave?

Besides all that, I had to find time to talk to Jess again about my idea of her sharing my grandma club. Wally and Amelia wanted to go on that walk soon, so I had to hope I could find Jess before they left. I sure had a lot to do on the last day of my vacation.

This time, I was ready for Jess. I had a list of my Shady Acres grandmas and a little note about each of them and what they were like. I kept that stuff safe and dry in a plastic bag on the porch while I played in the snow with Daddy again.

When he needed to go inside and watch football, I got my plastic bag and looked for Jess—who was outside just when I needed her to be. Maybe she had been watching me and Daddy and feeling jealous again.

I hoped she was in a good mood as I trudged through deep and then deeper snow. When I got close to that line she had drawn yesterday, I said, "Hi."

"Hi."

"I have a grandma club."

She got a squinty look in her eyes right away. I hoped I wasn't having bad timing with my great idea. Maybe she didn't want to talk about grandmas very much because she was still too sad about losing hers.

"They aren't my relatives, except for one, who is my great-grandma who is one hundred," I said anyway.

Jess only said, "Oh," about that.

"They live in a place called Shady Acres in my town. I visit them a lot. We have parties and I always make them letters and cards or pictures for their bulletin boards."

She didn't say anything at all. She just waited for me to tell her what in the world any of that had to do with her and her life.

"The thing is, they *love* to get letters!" I said. "And they love to get as many new friends as possible—especially girls like us."

Jess's eyes maybe got a little less squinty at me when I said "us," but she still didn't say anything back.

"The point is, if you wanted to, you could make one of them—or a couple of them, or a bunch of them or even *all* of them—happier by being a friend. To them." I waited and waited. That girl was hard to read, like a book in a different language. "If you like to write letters or draw or color or any of that stuff, you could share. With them. If you wanted. They also like, you know, bracelets made out of beads, and good jokes, and . . . stuff." When I handed her the plastic bag I was surprised that she took it. "This is the address. They all have the same one. And my mom and I wrote their names down, too, plus what they are like. For one example, Grandma Rose loves parakeets with me, but also she likes to talk about mysteries. Grandma Lucy is my friend Penny's relative and also she loves Elvis kind of a lot. Most of them love Elvis. Do you know who that is?"

"Elvis Presley?"

"Exactly. I guess I'm the only person who didn't know about him—until I did. I mean, I know about him now. I learned about him at Halloween." Now I could see that Jess was almost smiling at me. "I know it isn't the same as having a grandma here with you," I said more quietly. "I mean, someone to hug and to see and talk to. But I mean, it's nice to have people in your life in *some* way, right? And it makes them so happy to have letters and stuff."

She actually nodded a little bit after I said that.

"Maybe you could give them a picture of you— like your school picture, you know? Those little bitty ones? Do you get those here like we do? Or maybe you could even come down to New Jersey sometime and meet them!" I waited for her to say something, but she didn't. I gave up and did a shrug. "I am not putting pressure on you to do this, so don't worry about it."

She said, "Okay," and put the plastic bag in her jacket. She stared at me for a while. Then said a surprising word: "Thanks."

It didn't seem like she was going to do more talking about the grandma club or anything else, so I blurted out, "Do you know how long Fluffy was in your family? Could he have been around back in the olden days when your family bought this house, like in the 1990s?"

She looked surprised and then confused. Then she shook her head about that and said, "Fluffy and me are almost the same age. Grandma got him when I was a baby."

"Oh."

"Why?"

I told her about the letter I found in Elizabeth's closet that had to be from twenty-five years ago. "Doesn't that sound like something Fluffy would do?"

"Grandma had another poodle before Fluffy," Jess said.

My mouth dropped right open on me. "She did?" I asked. I tried not to sound super excited because I didn't want to scare Jess with too much of that.

"She was Fluffy's mom."

"Oh my *gosh!*" I said, giving her a startle even though I had just tried not to do that (oops!). "Do you know if Fluffy's mom stole mail too?"

Jess got a smile for real that time, but only because she thought that was a funny idea. Then she shrugged and said she didn't know.

"Maybe Fluffy learned to steal mail because of his mom! Maybe his mom was his teacher or trainer about that!"

"Maybe," she almost giggled. "Could've been."

I started giggling too, because I was imagining a white poodle mom teaching her poodle baby to do that stuff. Before long, we were both giggling kind of a lot. That was a real good thing for Rosalie to see when she came out of the big house. Moms like to see their kids being happy. "Jessie?" she called.

"I'm not over the line!" Jess called back. She sounded grouchy again and stopped those giggles real fast. "She came over here," she said, pointing her mitten at me. "I didn't do anything."

"We were having a funny talk," I said. "About the poodle stealing mail. Like, about how maybe Fluffy's mom taught him how to do that stuff."

Jess's mom smiled and shook her head about that. "Oh, isn't that *funny*?"

"Totally funny!" I agreed. "So do you think Fluffy learned to do that from his mom?"

Rosalie's smile got bigger . . . and then she *nodded*!

"Really?" Jess and I said together.

"Oh! I guess I never told you that story," she said to her daughter.

"Would you tell it now?" I asked.

"Okay. Sure. It's a short story. I actually saw it happen with my own eyes," Rosalie said. "I was walking the floors with Jessie," she pointed to Jess, "who was a fussy baby that morning, and then I saw Grandma's dogs, both Fluffy and his mom, running across the living room with mail in their mouths! They were as pleased as punch with themselves, those crazy dogs," Rosalie laughed.

I said, "Oh my gosh!"

Then Rosalie bent down to kiss her daughter's head. "We need to head to town to get some things for dinner, honey. Okay? You'll have time to talk more with Molly later."

Jess looked at me one more time and said "thanks" again before she turned to follow her mom to their car.

"What was the mom poodle's name?" I called after them.

Rosalie stopped walking and said, "Hmmm." Then she smiled and said, "Her name was Princess Opal."

"I never knew that," Jess said.

"That's because Grandma always just called her Opal," her mom said. "Come on, let's get going. See you later, Molly!

Chapter Eighteen
P and *O*

Princess Opal. *Princess Opal?!* I could hardly believe another *P* and *O* had just dropped on my head! I mean, suddenly I had *P* and *O* stuff coming out of my ears on me!

Okay, so it totally *was* the mom poodle who stole Evelyn's letter twenty-five years ago and hid it in Elizabeth's closet. Had to be. And that made sense. Well, it didn't really, but it made as much sense as poodles stealing mail could make.

I supposed it also made sense that the letter got left behind. Elizabeth and her family moved out real fast. It was a big surprise to her that they were even going. Nobody would have checked that closet too much for a possible letter way in the back. I mean, who would think of that? And so it stayed there and stayed there and stayed there in the dark back where nobody likes to go too much. Wow. That mystery felt pretty solved to me.

All that was left was for Amelia to tell her sister this stuff and see what happened next. That was totally up to her and none of my business, I thought.

"Well, just as I imagined," Amelia said, "Evelyn says she doesn't care about an old lost letter. She said to throw it away or read it if I was curious."

"Are you curious?" I asked.

Amelia nodded. "And hopeful, too. Whatever Evie says, I believe it *will* make a difference. Well, here goes. . . ."

Dear Evie,

I loved our time together and wish you could be here all the time. It is boring in this house out in the middle of the country with nobody to talk to except my parents. I hope you are feeling better about the break-up. Someone much better will come along. I am sure of it! You deserve a much better guy than Stuart, in my opinion. Not that I met him, but I think I can imagine him from what you said.

When are you coming back? Please tell me it won't be all the way in December! I don't think I can stand to wait that long. Obviously, I can't even wait to get your address first before writing this letter. I will finish up and put it in an envelope, then wait to hear from you first . . .

The letter went on and on about teenager girl stuff from the old days: bands and singers from a million years ago that I'd never even heard of, TV shows (same) and clothes and makeup. Those two were teenagers just like I thought Sophie would be (but she isn't). So weird to think of Evelyn being like that. I guess I have said that enough times, right? (But if you had met Evelyn and saw her in that fur coat, you would know why it is making so freaked out.)

Amelia folded the letter up real carefully and put it back in the envelope. There weren't any tears in her eyes this time. "I am going to find Elizabeth Danby," she said, and boy oh boy did she mean it. "And I am going to explain to her about the lost letters. And then I am going to give her my sister's phone number and let her get in touch. If she wants to. Oh, Molly—I really, really hope she wants to."

"Are you ready, darling?" Wally had his coat on and was holding Amelia's out to her. "Miss Molly, we are going to walk all around the property this morning. We will re-live some of Amelia's best memories of this place. Thank you in advance for watching the boys while we are out. We shouldn't be terribly long; it is quite chilly out there."

"No problem. You guys have fun. Make a snowman or whatever you want," I said. "I'll keep the guys busy and out of trouble."

"Ah. Yes," Wally chuckled. "But I am willing to bet that it is you who will be kept busy, and as far as trouble . . . we shall see."

"They're so quiet right now that it seems like they're not even around," I said. "They didn't fall asleep on me again, did they?"

Wally pointed toward the dining room. "Eating," he said, shaking his head. "I have also prepared a bag of treats for when they beg you for some—to save you and your mother the trouble this time."

"Thanks!"

"Perhaps some exercise would do them good," he added. "They have been eating an awful lot these past few days. Even though it is all healthy, of course, they still would benefit from some movement."

"Oh yes, but please watch them," Amelia said, sounding a little nervous. "I know it is only us in the house, but I still worry about them walking around in a strange place. Pip could so easily get lost, the way he darts about without—"

"I will watch them *super* carefully," I promised. "Don't worry about a single thing. Have fun!"

Chapter Nineteen
Looking for Lost Mail

Teddy and Pip had sure liked playing Hide and Treat in Elizabeth's room, and they liked the other games on this vacation, too. I thought it would be a great idea to make another game out of looking for the lost piece of mail. This time, I could hide stuff in lots more places—all downstairs. Lucky for me, Wally had put together that bag of veggies, so all I had to do was hide them.

Daddy was on the case upstairs—and I didn't even need to hide treats for that help (tee hee!). Mostly, I wanted him to look real hard in Elizabeth's closet. I mean, even though the letter from Evelyn was put there by Fluffy's mom, Princess Opal (I still couldn't believe the dog's name was *P* and *O*!), she could've taught her baby to put stuff in there, too.

So anyway, I hid treats all over the place downstairs, looking for lost mail while I did that.

Teddy and Pip waited for me (not one bit patiently) in the travel cage by the window. They were getting really noisy and probably making it hard for Mom to have any peace, so I started to hide the treats faster.

"Okay, okay! I'm done!" I finally called.

"Molly Jane, we are wanting to do something and not only sit and scream in this travel cage!"

"WE ARE BORED! WE WOULD LIKE TO BE SECRET JET EYE NIGHTS OR CLUE-FINDING DETECTIVE DUDES! ONLY SITTING IN THIS TEENY AND ALSO TINY PLACE IS NO FUN AND NO GOOD! OUT OUT OUT OUT!"

"I know, and I'm sorry. I was making a fun detective treats game, and it took a while," I said as I lifted Teddy out. "I hid treats all over the downstairs. All you have to do is find them. And while you're looking, please check for lost mail too, okay? I am really counting on your help today!"

"Molly Jane, Teddy is on your case! Here he goes! To the rescue!"

"Thanks, buddy!" I smiled as Teddy waddled off, starting his hunt right under the dining room table.

"Remember not to chew on the Christmas tree or any needles that fell off!"

"Molly Jane, Teddy knows not to chew that stuff. It is no good. I want to eat only good treats."

"PIP IS BORED AND WANTS TO BE OUT! OUT OUT OUT!"

"Okay, here you go," I said. After I lifted him, I held on for a little bit, even though he was very squirmy. "I am leaving the litter box right here on the floor by the table, okay? And please make noises sometimes so I know where you are! Unless you want to stick together . . . ?"

"I would like to not stick to that Pip for a time," Teddy called. *"Okay, Molly Jane? Okay! Over and over and out and out!"*

I finally set Pip on the floor and said, "Please? Make noises so I know where you are?"

"ORRIE VWAH, MOLLY JANE!" is what he said. Then he took off like a little rocket, singing loud for all to hear.

> *Finding treats in a*
> *Haunted house downstairs*
> *Sneaky sneaking round and round.*
> *Molly Jane hides them,*
> *Pip and Teddy find them—*
> *Best and worst of times all in one!*
> *CRUNCH!*

> *Finding treats in a*
> *Haunted house downstairs*
> *Sneaky sneaking round and round.*
> *Lettuce (YUM!), broccoli (YUM!)*
> *And carrots, too (YUM YUM)!*
> *Best and worst of times all in one!*
> *CRUNCH!*

"Don't forget to look for mail, too!" I called after him.

"MAIL, SNAIL, PAIL, JAIL! PIP SAVES THE DAY!"

When Daddy walked into the room shaking his head, it was not a good sign. "Nothing," he said.

"Really?"

"Really."

"Rats. But thanks for checking."

"You are welcome."

"I'd better not let these guys get too far away from me. See ya later!"

Finding treats and mail in a
Haunted house downstairs
Sneaky sneaking round and round . . .

I could still hear Pip singing, so I knew he wasn't far and was okay. Whew.

I needed to listen harder to find Teddy. I didn't hear him at all, and that made me nervous. "Teddy? Sweetie? Make some noise for me so I know where you are, okay?" Maybe this game in the big downstairs wasn't a good idea after all. Maybe I should've done it one room at a time. "Teddy?" I called again.

I was so relieved when that cute black head appeared in the kitchen doorway. *"Molly Jane, I am finding treats and eating them. That is what Teddy is doing. Have no worries, friend. Here I am. Did you miss your friend Teddy?"*

"Yes!" I sat on the floor by him and pet him for a while. "I sure did. Are you finding lots of treats?"

"Some. Not all, I am thinking. I am hoping to find more of those crunchy things."

"Did you see any mail?"

"I did look for mail—yes, I did—but only treats are coming to me. That is okay with your friend Teddy for now! Tee hee! Treats are better than mail, unless mail is from a best friend; then it is very good

stuff. Is the mail you speak of from a best friend, Molly Jane?"

"The mail is from the daddy of the girl who used to live here. He is far away and she misses him a ton. So . . . yes."

"Yes, I know of that missing. My friend Wally was gone far away one time for a very long time. That is when I met Amelia, who is a friend too. Sometimes the friends go away and Pip and me are watched over by other friends. We like all best friends together. That is what we prefer."

"Yeah. I know."

"All best friends are together at this place, except not Max and not our friend Sophie."

"Look, the reason I want to look so hard for mail is because I hope Jess's dad sent something for Christmas. I have big hopes that the poodle stole it and hid it somewhere."

"Poodle is a silly sil, Molly Jane! Teddy says Bad Barbara stole mail. She does that stuff. We know it."

"Well, this time it seems like Fluffy is the one who did it instead. Barbara is far away in New Jersey—I promise. Again."

"I don't know, Molly Jane. Maybe. Maybe not. Barbara is still the one Teddy thinks did it."

"Anyway, if nobody stole anything, that means Jess's dad didn't send a single thing for Christmas. That is much worse, I think. That is too sad to even think about!"

"Yes, it is sad indeed. Pip and me had a Christmas that was sad like that, one time. Amelia was Bridezilla, and Wally did not live at our house so

far. There were no lights and there was no tree. No presents, no jingles. Until Molly Jane and Dad brought that stuff to us. And then it got better and better. We had our Christmas at your house, Molly Jane, and a wedding too! It was good. I do not want this girl to be sadder than sad, so I will now look and look for this thing you are thinking is lost in this big haunted house. Except please tell me the very poodle who maybe steals mail is not in this house too, or also, or anymore. Okay? He will not eat us guinea pigs all up, right, Molly Jane?! He did not already crunch up that Pip, right?!"

"No, of course not! Fluffy lives in the house next door and is for sure not in this house now. I promise. I would never let you be out and running around if he was." I pet Teddy some more and smiled into his cute little face. "You're safe. So is Pip."

"Okay. That is good news. I will go now and look for mail and more treats, too. Molly Jane, you are possibly and probably needing to check on the doings of that crazy guinea pig called Pip now anyway. He will find trouble if there is some to find."

"Okay. You're right."

"Truly."

"Thanks for reminding me, buddy!" I jumped up to my feet. "See you later! Pip? Where are you?" I called.

I listened hard. Then I heard squeaky singing somewhere. Whew! If he was singing, Pip was fine. And that meant that while I looked for him, I had to time to look for lost mail, too.

I looked *all over the place*: behind things and under things, in places I had already looked twice—but nothing. What a crazy mystery, huh?

"Molly Jane! Molly Jane Fisher! Over and over and where are you?!"

"Teddy? Are you okay?"

"Yes! It is Teddy saying that stuff with no walkie or talkie to talk to! Come over! It is good news, not bad!"

"It's good news? Really?! Keep talking so I can find you!"

"Talking talking talking. Teddy is talking and talking, and I hear foots coming now that are probably from the feet of Molly Jane Fisher . . ."

I followed Teddy's voice into the laundry room, which was right behind the kitchen. I had not been in there this morning hiding a treat. I was sure of it. "Did you find something in here?"

"Maybe or maybe not. Teddy sees a paper-y something, Molly Jane. Look!" Teddy walked slowly toward the crack between the dryer and the wall. After a quick peek, he zoomed back to stand by me. *"I do not prefer it back there, Molly Jane!"*

"I know what you mean," I agreed.

"Fuzz and fuzz and other stuff I do not know about. Furry gray fuzz is there, and I am afraid of that stuff. I think it is monster fluff and would prefer not to see it. Anymore. But also, I think there is maybe a piece of mail for you to see. But only if you are too not too afraid to look. Maybe Dad Dan can do the looking."

"I think I can handle it," I said.

"Okay, Molly Jane. But be careful."

Teddy was sure right about the dust and fluff and fuzz back there. (It was like that behind our dryer, too. Yuck.) I could see something else, though, and—*yes!* It was a piece of paper, maybe a piece of mail. Maybe it was something totally awesome!

But first I had to get it out of there, and that wouldn't be easy. My arm was too short to just grab it, so I looked around for something to use. I found a hanger. It was tough, but moving real slowly, I pushed the mail against the wall and moved the hanger up and up until—bingo! I grabbed it with my hand and held on tight.

And, well, it sure *was* a piece of lost mail, but it wasn't a letter. I brushed off the dusty fluff to see what it exactly was (yuck!) and found out that what it was, was junk mail. Darn it. I knew junk mail when I saw it. It was addressed to "Resident" instead of the people who lived there.

But, I told myself, finding a piece of junk mail with a postage date of just before Christmas meant we were on the right track. That was the bright side. There was still lots of hope about finding the important mail. Maybe Fluffy hid one thing behind the dryer and other things somewhere else. So we had to keep looking.

I set the junk mail on the dryer and wiped my hands off on my jeans. "Good job, Teddy! You get the first point and a shiny gold star!"

Teddy purred as I pet him.

"Come on, let's find some more!"

"Hooray for Teddy! You will tell that crazy Pip that Teddy found the mail that saved the day, right, Molly Jane? Right?"

"Yes. Of course I will. Now keep going, buddy! Find some more! I'd better find Pip."

"Yes indeed, Molly Jane! You'd better!"

"Pip?!" I called. I had a little shiver of worry. I mean, I was one hundred percent responsible for those guys right now, wasn't I? That was a lot of responsible to have on my shoulders, and I had no idea where Pip even was in this big house!

I headed to the kitchen first, because that was the last place I heard him singing. But the kitchen was empty and I also couldn't hear the singing anymore. My heart started beating kind of a lot, and I felt a little sweaty, even though it was cold and December. "Pip! Sweetie? Where are you?!"

Chapter Twenty
Mom Jane Saves . . . Pip?

Were you worried? I was too. It was way too quiet, and it seemed like Pip was nowhere to be found. The Hide and Treat for Mail game was looking like a real bad idea by then, and I wished I wasn't the person in charge of everything. "Pip? Where *are* you? Please sing or scream or something, okay? Please?"

And then, suddenly . . . whoa. *Huh?!* There was Pip, in the last place in the whole wide world I would ever dream of seeing that little guy: in my mom's arms.

Yeah, I know! It was so amazing and strange that I had to shake myself to wake up, in case I was dreaming. Nope. I was awake.

Mom, walking real slow and careful, came right into the living room by me with Pip cradled in her arms.

And he wasn't screaming or anything! I mean, Pip was all the way quiet—like, one hundred and ten percent quiet.

"What happened?" I asked, and my voice was a whispery shocked whisper.

"Well, I was heading into the powder room," Mom said with one eyebrow up, "and this one came zooming in. Apparently he had gotten himself lost."

I looked at Pip, who stayed one hundred and ten percent quiet about that. "I should've been watching him better," I whispered.

"He's fine. But he hasn't said a word," Mom said. "Which is okay with me," she added. Then she kind of smiled. Mom would prefer it if Teddy and Pip never did their human talk. A quiet Pip was her kind of Pip.

"Hi, Pip," I said. "I'm sorry I wasn't watching you better."

Pip made a little sound that almost sounded like a little purr. Except that would be too amazing to even stand, right?

"I'll take him," I said to Mom. "Thank you *so much* for taking care of him!"

She shook her head. Then she shook it some more. "You're welcome. Here you go." Mom handed Pip to me and then did another amazing thing to add to the big pile of other Christmas miracles: she reached out her hand and gave Pip a little scratch behind his ears. "See you later," she said to him.

Chapter Twenty-one
A New Plan

Whoa. That was *so* amazing I had to give it its own chapter! (I hope you don't mind.)

"Do you want to talk about it?" I asked Pip.

He stayed quiet and super-weirdly calm, even now that Mom was out of the room.

"Are you okay?"

"MOLLY JANE, WE WILL NOT TALK OF IT," Pip whispered. *"OKAY? OKAY. NOT TO TEDDY SO FAR. OR MAYBE NOT EVER."*

"You need some time to think about it, huh?" I guessed. "I get it. It takes a while for our minds to catch up with amazing things that happen. Like me and Benny Nubb, for one example."

"NUBB NUBB NUBB, BLUB BLUB BLUB?"

"Exactly."

"MOM JANE WAS NOT NO GOOD," Pip whispered. *"NOT TO THIS PIP. NOT THIS TIME. SO FAR. TO PIP. TODAY."*

I smiled and kissed his little head. "I know. Know what else? I think she likes you."

Pip shook his little head and whispered, *"MAYBE."*

"Well, did you find any mail when you were running so far away from me?"

"*NO. NOT MAIL. SOME TREATS, BUT NO MYSTERY MAIL. PIP FINDS A SMALLISH ROOM THAT HAS A P.U. TOILET IN IT, BUT THERE WAS NO MYSTERY MAIL BY THAT THING.*"

"Thanks for checking."

"*NOW SAY TO ME THAT TEDDY FRIEND DID NOT FIND MAIL TOO OR EITHER, OKAY?! PIP WILL SAVE THIS DAY AND ALL THE DAYS FOR MOLLY JANE!*"

"Let's find him," I said. "And then I think we'd better stick together. This place is too big and full of hiding places, and I don't want to lose you guys!"

"*STICKY STICKING WITH ALL BEST FRIENDS TOGETHER DOES SOUND RIGHT AND GOOD, EVEN TO PIP WHO SAVES THE DAY. PIP MAYBE DID GO TOO FAR, AND THEN THERE WAS MOM JANE . . .*" But Pip did not seem to know how to finish what he was going to say.

"Yeah. I get it. Teddy? Where are you, buddy?" I called. "I found Pip, and now we're going to look for clues together. Please make some sounds so I can find you!"

I was so relieved when his sweet face poked out from behind a lamp table near the fireplace. "*Nice day, Molly Jane? Pip, is this weather okay for you?*"

"*PIP IS OKAY. PIP IS GOING TO GET DOWN NOW AND LOOK FOR MYSTERY CLUE MAIL. MOLLY JANE? I WOULD LIKE TO BE THE PLACE CALLED 'DOWN'.*"

After I set Pip on the floor, he started running around like crazy. Except he stayed right in the living room, and he also kept checking over his shoulder to be sure I was still there.

"I won't leave you. I promise," I said.

"MOLLY JANE, BAD BARBARA IS NOT HIDING THE MAIL, RIGHT? SAY THAT IS RIGHT!"

"For sure she isn't."

"MAIL MAIL MAIL MAIL! WHERE EVEN ARE YOU, CRAZY MAIL? WHY ARE YOU BEING IN THE SLIPPERY-SLOPPY MOUTH OF A POODLE DOG AND THEN HIDEY-HIDING FROM YOUR HUMAN FRIENDS? THAT IS NO GOOD, MAIL! COME OUT AND COME OVER AND OVER! THE END!"

"Crazy Pip, mail is not a person who knows of talking. You cannot tell it what to do."

"MAIL?! WHERE ARE YOU, MAIL?! MOLLY JANE, THERE IS NO MAIL!"

Pip was starting to get all freaked out, and I kind of was too. I had looked so many places! There had to be something, but where could it *be*?!

Then I decided to stop freaking out and do some thinking instead. *Think, Molly!*

I sat on a chair near the fireplace, and the guys stood on the floor by my feet. Where in the world could or would Fluffy hide letters (besides behind the dryer) that I hadn't already looked?

I had no idea.

I had looked everywhere.

"Guys? We need a plan."

"Yes, a plan is good. But firstly, Molly Jane, friend, Teddy would like very much to have a drink and maybe also some hay. Thank you!"

"PIP NEEDS TO DO HIS POTTY!"

"Right. Sorry. I need to take better care of you guys! Let's have our meeting about the plan by the travel cage," I said.

After both guinea pigs did some business, they rested up and munched hay while I talked through the clues and problems. "Let's try to think about where a dog who steals mail would take a stack of letters in this house, okay?"

"DOGS HAVE BIG SCARY MOUTHS!"

"Molly Jane, sorry, but we cannot know what dogs are thinking, exactly, in those dog minds."

"No, I guess not." I thought for another while. "I think what I need to do is to trace Fluffy's steps."

"WHAT ARE YOU SAYING, MOLLY JANE?!"

"Trace? What means trace?"

"It means I need to figure out where the mail came into the house and where it maybe got set down. Then I'll know where it was when Fluffy grabbed it. If I know that, maybe I can try to guess where he might have gone with it."

The guinea pigs stared at me and chewed hay.

"You guys are okay staying right there for a while, right? I'll be in the living room, and then I'll be right back! Just call if you need me!" I knew they would be totally fine up there in the cage—much finer than if they were running all over on the floor like before. I actually felt nervous, looking backward, because of almost losing Pip like that. Good thing Mom was around! Seeing her with Pip in her arms like that was so amaz—

Oh my gosh, the front door had a mail chute!

Chapter Twenty-two
Teddy and Pip Save the Day

Do you know why a mail chute made me excited? A mail chute means the mail gets shoved in and then falls right on the floor in a little pile. That means a dog like Fluffy would have an easy time of taking it and hiding it around the house. It also means it makes sense that he did that and that he *probably* did that. Maybe he thought the mail at this house was a toy for him (or else a whole pile of toys) to drag around.

I could see it in my imagination, too. The mail came popping through the chute one busy day. Fluffy was close by. He was the only one who saw it come in, and he thought it was a fun pile of toys. He grabbed it, just like he'd seen his mom do back in the olden days, and then . . . ?

That was the question, wasn't it? *Then* what did he do with it?

I did more imagination and saw him playing with it a bit. Then, after he played with it, where did he bring it? I didn't know. I couldn't figure it out.

Was it possible that there was only that one piece of junk mail that day? Fluffy jumped up on the dryer with it and dropped it behind, and that was that?

Except it was Christmastime! People get more mail at Christmas than usual, right? There had to be more!

Where did Fluffy *put* it?

It had to be low, like, not very high up from the ground, I guessed. Even if a poodle could jump high, like up onto a dryer, maybe he wouldn't try it with a stack of mail in his mouth. I am for sure not an expert at dogs, so I can't know.

I decided to do some assuming that Fluffy would not do a big jump, but would drop the mail someplace low when he was tired of playing with it.

I turned away from the door and looked around the living room real slowly. I had hidden treats all over the place in there—in every place I thought of—and the guinea pigs had found them all but hadn't found any mail.

I crouched down so I was shorter, like as short as Fluffy was, or closer to it. Where would I go if I had mail in my little mouth and wanted to put it down so I could play with it later?

"Guys? I think I have a job made for guinea pigs," I said. I explained what I wanted them to do.

"MOLLY JANE, WHAT ARE YOU SAYING?!" Pip squeaked at me. *"YOU ARE SAYING TO US THAT YOU WANT TEDDY AND ME—WHO ARE GUINEA PIGS—TO DO A PRETEND AND BE A POODLE? NO GOOD! NO THANK YOU! NO NO!"*

Teddy shook his head at Pip. *"Pip, we are being mystery detective spies, that is all. We are thinking with our feet about where to go if we have* been stealing mail or playing with mail like that silly dog was maybe doing. Do not be more silly than the fluffy fluff poodle."

"Right," I said. "Exactly. So, okay, here you go." I set Teddy by the front door and then got Pip and set him there too.

Teddy started a slow walk away from the front door, and Pip followed so close that he bumped into him.

"Crazy Pip, please give your friend some room to move his feet. Here," Teddy said, stopping by the coffee table. *"Here is one place that Teddy would go to be sneaky or to drop stuff he stole out of his very mouth. If ever he did that stuff. Which he would not do."*

I tried reaching under the coffee table from every side until, "Oh! Oh my gosh, guys! There's something under here!"

"Oh our gosh, too, Molly Jane!"

"WHAT IS IT?! WHAT?! WHAT?! IS BAD BARBARA UNDER THAT TABLE?!"

"Of course not, Pip. But I know there's something made out of paper under there . . ." It was too far under for me to grab, so I sat up and looked around a bit. The fireplace poker looked like something I maybe shouldn't touch, but it would also be a good thing to use for something just like this.

I made sure it was clean and wouldn't hurt the rug, and then I used it to push the thing out. It was so exciting . . . until I pulled it out and looked at it. Oh. It was just like the other piece of mail: nothing important—just a bill or whatever.

"Good job, Teddy," I said anyway, because he sure did find a piece of mail (again!) and deserved a gold star.

"BUT PIP IS THE ONE WHO SAVES THE DAY, MOLLY JANE! PIP FOUND IT!"

"And Pip," I added.

"Except for that Pip only followed and tripped on Teddy's feet. That was no help. Teddy found that thing. That is truth."

I put the fireplace poker back, sat on the floor, and tried to think again. "Where else, guys? It looks like Fluffy left or dropped his pile of mail all over the place instead of all in one spot, right? Or maybe he hid the other things other days and there is still the jackpot of mail to find. I hope."

"GUESS SO. MAYBE SO. WHAT ARE YOU SAYING, MOLLY JANE?"

"It looks like that is true, Molly Jane. One drop here, one there. Maybe that is all, but maybe there is still a pot of jacks."

I squeezed my head between my hands. "There *has* to be more! A daddy would not skip sending a present or at least a card to his daughter on Christmas!"

Teddy did a big yawn and rested his head on his paws. *"I am sad to say this, but maybe the Grinch stole the Christmas from that girl."*

"FRIENDS, PIP WILL NOW SAVE THIS DAY. DO NOT BE SAD OR THINKING THIS IS THE END OF THE MAIL."

"What are you going to do, Pip?"

"SAVE THE DAY," Pip said again.

"Well, okay. Go ahead!"

"MOLLY JANE, TELL PIP WHAT HE NEEDS TO DO AND HE WILL DO IT!"

"Crazy Pip. Molly Janes needs for you to have ideas. That is how you save the day."

"How about if you start by the door and pretend you are carrying mail? Just run wherever you would go without thinking first."

"PIP IS NOW A SILLY SILLY POODLE DOG, AND HE HAS MAIL IN HIS VERY MOUTH. PIP WANTS TO BE SNEAKY AND TRICKY AND MAKE THE HUMANS NOT HAVE THEIR MAIL. WHICH IS NOT NICE. PIP WOULD NOT DO THAT STUFF. OKAY, HERE IS THE SHINING NIGHT OF THE GUINEA PIGS, AND HE IS NOW FINDING THE MAIL FOR MOLLY JANE! READY? READY!"

"Wait!" Teddy waddled quickly to the door. *"Teddy will do this! Teddy is being the silly poodle too or instead of that Pip!"*

Well, that did it. Racing each other, and probably not thinking except about who would "win" or save the day first, they took off like little furry rockets—away from the door and right to . . . the Christmas tree?

Chapter Twenty-three
What We Found Behind the Tree

"*HERE! HERE IS WHERE THE SILLY POODLE GOES!*" Pip called. "*HERE IS HIS SNEAKY SPOT, MOLLY JANE FISHER! CASE CLOSED! THE END! PIP SAVES THE DAY!*"

"*Yes, it is truly true! There is more mail back here, Molly Jane! Come over and over to see! Over?*"

My heart was pounding like a big drum as I got closer. Yep, behind the beautiful tree, up against the wall and mixed in with the pretend presents, was a little stack of mail with a rubber band around it. Whoa and yay!

Teddy and Pip started pulling, pushing, and tugging at it, trying to get it closer to me.

"It's okay, guys. I'll climb under there and get it. Wow, you two are *totally* solving the mystery. I am super-duper grateful!" It was tricky to get back there. I had to be real careful not to knock anything over—the whole tree, for one example. I also had to be careful with those ornaments.

When I finally got into a spot where I could sit down, I picked up the stack of mail and looked it over. There were definitely little dog teeth marks on the top envelope. Fluffy for sure had done this! Oh my gosh, this was *so cool*, and Jess and Rosalie would be so happy!

The "from" address on the top letter was someone who lived in "VT"—that is Vermont. I guessed that it was a Christmas card from the red envelope. It wasn't from a different country, from Jess's Dad, but it was going to make them happy to get the lost card, no matter who it was from. I put that one on the floor and looked at the next one.

I got real excited when I saw "Ellington" in that "from" spot, but then I read the first name. It was Dorothy. She had sent that thing from somewhere in New York. I set that one down, too.

There were only two things left in the stack, and the next one was junk mail. Darn it.

Only one more. . . .

Rats! The last piece of stolen mail in the rubber-banded-together bunch was only some advertising thing about a sale at a jewelry store. "Is this for *sure* all there was?" I asked Teddy and Pip. I felt kind of crushed. "Are you sure there aren't any other letters back there?"

"Molly Jane, I will look some more, but I think that is all. I have looked and looked already and I see only presents here and there. My feelings will not hurt so much if you look too. Go ahead. It is alright."

"It's not that I don't believe you," I said. "It's just . . ." I didn't finish the sentence. "I just have to look." I searched around and under all the presents under that tree.

Nothing.

"Maybe he left a *different* pile somewhere else on a different day," I said, even though I didn't really think so. I was losing hope about the whole thing by then. I had already looked everywhere in the whole downstairs—everywhere that was low enough for a poodle to hide mail. I was sure of it. And I trusted that Daddy had looked super well upstairs, too.

It was probably confusing for my dad when he walked in and found me slumping behind the Christmas tree. "What's going on?" he asked. "Hey, guys," he said to the guinea pigs.

"HELLO, DAD! HOW IS YOUR WEATHER? PIP IS DOING MANNERS AT YOU NOW. GOOD ONES."

"Dad Dan, we are doing the sad because we found the mail but it is not the right mail. Molly Jane hoped for it to be more or different or better mail, but it is not those things."

I carefully climbed back out of that weird spot for sitting. Teddy and Pip followed me.

"Really? That's too bad," Daddy sighed for me. "I'm sorry to hear that." Then he gave me a hug, which helped a lot. "Well, no one can say you didn't give it your very best shot, kiddo."

"I guess they couldn't. Not fairly. We worked really hard, me and the guys. Teddy and Pip were awesome!" I heard both of them purring after I said that.

"I know—let's see if there are some cookies around here," Daddy said. "Some hot chocolate, too. And maybe something for the guys."

"YES! YES, THANK YOU, DAD!"

"Please and thank you!"

"You guys!" I said. "You have been eating *all day.*"

Daddy found a couple little carrots for Teddy and Pip anyway. Then he microwaved some water for us. He poured it over hot chocolate powder in the Santa mugs while I brought the whole plastic bowl of Mom's cookies and some napkins to the dining room table.

"MOLLY JANE? TEDDY AND ME ARE DONE CRUNCHING AND NOW WOULD LIKE TO PLAY VADER! YOU ARE VADER, OKAY? OKAY!"

"Best friend Molly Jane, we will play the thing of hide and seek from Vader. Okay?"

"Sure. Okay. But please stay in the living room, the dining room, or maybe the kitchen. Don't go too far. I'll count to fifty and then come looking for you."

Daddy agreed to be my spy so I wouldn't lose track of them all over again. And while I was supposed to be counting to fifty, I told him what was going on with the mystery of Jess's dad's letter.

Daddy only said, "Ah."

I handed him the pile of mail and he looked through it, nodding. He did a little sigh and handed it back. "You had your hopes up," he said.

"Real high."

"Well, I looked everywhere I could think of," he said. "And I am sure you did too."

"I looked everywhere except behind the tree, I guess. Or under the coffee table. Teddy and Pip looked those places and found stuff."

"They'll be glad to get what you found," Daddy said. "Even if it isn't what you were hoping for. She'll even be glad for this electric bill."

"I doubt it. Okay, guys, where are you?" I called.

Daddy nodded at the coffee table and mouthed, "Teddy," then he sneakily pointed a thumb at the china cabinet and mouthed "Pip."

To be fair, I pretended to take a while to find them. Pip ran squealing away from me, saying, *"BEW BEW!"* over his shoulder, like we were having a blaster battle. *"DAD DAN! IT IS VADER AND HE IS GOING TO GET YOU! RUN RUN RUN FROM MOLLY JANE VADER! BEW BEW!"*

Daddy only laughed about that and had another cookie.

"Don't go too far, Pip!" I called. Then I found Teddy and scooped him up and carefully hugged him. "Hi, sweetie."

"Hi, Molly Jane! Surprise! Here I am! I will not run from you. I know you are not Vader. Pip likes to be crazy, so we will let him scream about that stuff." Teddy licked my hand.

Well, we did a couple more turns at the sort-of-Vader game until Teddy yawned and even Pip looked a little tired. Pip usually does not do tired, so I knew I had worn those two out.

"I'd better get them back in the cage," I told Daddy. "Oh, how are your allergies?"

He smiled and shook his head. "No problems. I took some medicine, and I'm fine."

"Daddy? Do you think Jess's dad really forgot all about her on Christmas? Would a dad *do* that?"

He shook his head for a while and then said, "I can't imagine it."

When they were in and happily munching hay (Pip) or napping (Teddy), I sat and thought more about the mysteries and Tweets' clue. It was for sure now that *P* and *O* was about that poodle mom named Princess Opal, right? She took Elizabeth's letter and hid it, and somehow Tweets knew about that.

P.O. does also mean mail, like, just plain mail—"post office," like Nora said. Maybe Tweets didn't know the name of the poodle from long ago. I mean, how could he? Maybe he just knew there was going to be a mystery about different lost pieces of mail.

I supposed that the other thing *P* and *O* could have meant was inviting Jess to join the grandma club by sending letters (through the *post office*), which I had already done.

Maybe the missing letter from Jess's dad wasn't even a mystery for me to try to solve. Maybe there wasn't a missing letter to be found.

Or maybe Tweets was talking about the missing junk mail that I *did* find.

I supposed I would never know for sure. Tweets and his clues are a big mystery all on their own.

Chapter Twenty-four
All Best Friends Together

"Hello, hello!" Wally and Amelia came in the front door, looking rosy from the walk in the cold weather and very happy, too. They liked this vacation time a whole lot. I could tell.

When they thanked me again for being there and watching the guys while they did things together, it made me feel pretty good and also made me forget a little how disappointed I felt about not finding a letter for Jess.

Teddy and Pip started up the usual excited talk and calling out for their best friends. The quiet house got totally noisy and full of . . . well, full of people who really loved each other. Lucky us, right? I counted my blessings, remembered I had a ton, and started to feel a whole lot better.

The back door opened, and then there was the sound of bags rustling. This made Teddy and Pip start up some wheeking and whooping (I don't think they can help that; it's instinct). "Hello?" Rosalie called. "I'm bringing in some things to go along with your dinner tonight! Sorry to disturb you!"

"Rosalie's here," Amelia said. "The boys!" she added and we all knew what she meant.

"Guinea pig sounds only!" Wally whispered to Teddy and Pip.

"I'll go talk to her," Amelia said as Wally rushed to the cage to make sure the guys didn't slip up at just the wrong second.

"Hey, didn't you want to give this to her?" Daddy was holding the little pile of mail that I had left on the table.

"Oh. Yeah. I guess," I shrugged. I had made up such a great picture in my head about how it would go when I gave her something a lot better than an electric bill, two cards from relatives, and three pieces of junk mail. The real thing would be pretty disappointing compared to that, but I followed Amelia into the kitchen anyway.

The ladies were starting a talk about what was for dinner.

"Hello, Molly," Rosalie said. "Jessie . . . is hard at work writing *letters* this afternoon! And I am *so* grateful to you for the idea."

"No problem," I shrugged.

"I think having pen-pal grandmas will make her a little less lonely, now that her grandma is gone."

"I hope so," I said.

"She plans, or hopes, to get the letters all finished in time for you to bring them with you and deliver them right to the ladies yourself. That'll save us some stamps," she added with a smile.

"I'd be real happy to be your mail carrier," I said, and I really meant that. My grandmas were going to love that *so* much! "I'll start that job now, I guess," I said. I handed her the little packet of mail. "The guinea pigs found these behind the Christmas tree," I said.

"The—? Behind the—?" Rosalie looked real confused. The way she flipped through the stack real fast made me sure she was hoping for more than what it was, just like I had been. Except her hope was huge, and so she had to be disappointed times a zillion.

"I was wondering about Dorothy's card," she said quietly. "And there's that electric bill!"

Huh. I guess she *was* excited about that. "I think maybe, probably, Fluffy took your mail one day and hid it. It was mixed in with the pretend presents," I said. "Behind the tree."

"And Teddy and Pip found these?" Amelia asked. "Oh my goodness!"

"We were playing a game, and . . . well, yeah, they found these." I decided to explain it better later, if Amelia really wanted me to.

"That crazy dog," Rosalie laughed. "Thank you, Molly."

"You're welcome," I shrugged.

"Well, I need to get back to my house," Rosalie said. "I will be back with your dinner at six o'clock. I am making something really special for your last night," she promised with a smile.

Amelia thanked her for that and for getting more lettuce, too. Then she walked with her to the door.

When the kitchen door was all the way shut, Amelia called, "All clear!"

The guinea pigs' whooping and wheeking turned into talking right away as the guys explained what we'd been up to all morning.

Of course, it sounded totally cuckoo and dangerous the way they told it, so I was glad to be there to explain and make it sound a little better and safer.

"So the mail was only mail and not the mystery that Molly Jane was hoping for," Teddy sighed.

"PIP SAVED THE DAY! PIP WAS THE ONE! PIP WAS THE POODLE AND FOUND THE MAIL! YES, HE DID! DO NOT SAY HE DID NOT!"

"Except this crazy Pip got lost in the bathroom before—remember that thing and time? And Pip got the rescue by the very person of Mom Jane!"

"NO NO! THAT IS NOT A TRUE STORY!"

Wally and Amelia were real interested in hearing about that, let me tell you. They even asked me to be a back-up for Teddy's story.

"Friends, you are maybe now hurting Teddy's feelings by saying his words are not true!"

"Sorry, Theodore," Wally said nicely, petting him. "It is, however, quite an amazing story."

"True. It is. I saw the thing. I spied and saw it. I was a sneaking spy and did not tell what I saw until just this time now."

"I saw it with these eyes, too," I said. "Mom carried him, real nice, into this room, and Pip was as quiet as . . . anything. It's all true."

"NO NO! MOM JANE . . . IT WAS NOT . . . PIP SAVED THE DAY! PIP WAS THE SHINY NIGHT OF ARMOR, NOT LOST IN A BATHROOM! NO NO!"

We all had to laugh about that a little, and that's what we were doing when Mom walked in. She gave us a "what's going on" kind of look as the guinea pigs got real quiet.

"Hi, Pip," Mom said (another miracle, I think). "Hello, Teddy."

"Nice . . . day . . . Mom Jane?" Teddy asked in a whisper.

Pip said a very, very quiet little "HI!" before he ran into an igloo, squealing his little head off.

Mom shook her smiling head and kept going toward the kitchen.

Teddy went back to the subject of who saved the day when she was out of sight. "Anyway, friends, the truly truth is that Teddy found the mail. Teddy found all of that stuff. Pip followed and bumped into Teddy and was in the way, mostly, but Teddy was the hero of the day. Remember, Molly Jane? Remember the first mail with the furry fluffs stuck on? Teddy found that, not Pip. Pip was busy being lost when that mail was found. Then Teddy found mail under the table with the fireplace stick . . ."

"That's right. Teddy did find the first piece of mail," I said. "Sorry, Pip, but it's true. He found two pieces before you both found the stack behind the tree."

"NO NO!" Pip called from the igloo. "PIP DID IT!"

"Molly Jane, friend, Teddy would like very much to know that the mail he, not Pip, found in that scary haunted furry-fluff place is now with the lady who maybe sometimes lives in this place. Teddy wants to know that his mail has made her very happy indeed. Because of Teddy being a hero. And saving the day."

Pip peeked his little face out and said, "EXCEPT PIP FOUND IT AND SAVED THE DAY!"

"I think that one is still in the laundry room, actually. Thanks for reminding me, Teddy! I'll go get it now. We can give it to her at dinnertime."

"I like the time called dinnertime. It is one of my favorite times."

"Me too," I said with a smile. "And I am so sure that she'll be very, very happy about that piece of mail you found. Good job, buddy. You found two very important things for Rosalie today."

Teddy did some happy purring while Pip yelled some more that he was the one who found it all and saved the day.

I don't know exactly why, but suddenly I felt real sleepy. "I'll get it now so I don't forget," I said with a yawn. I peeked in the laundry room and saw the piece of junk mail on the dryer where I'd left it. It still had a little bit of dryer fuzz on it, too. I got a paper towel from the kitchen and started to wipe it off for Rosalie. I did the first side, turned it over . . . and then the most amazing thing happened.

Chapter Twenty-five
Post Office

That piece of junk mail was not *only* a piece of junk mail. When I turned it over to wipe dryer gunk off of the other side, I saw a sticker. It was like a post-it note sticker stuck on there, but it shouldn't have been stuck on there, I don't think. I looked harder and knew that it was not a regular post-it note sticker either. The sticker was from the . . . *POST OFFICE!*

I was so excited I kind of yelled for everyone to come quick. I probably scared them all kind of a lot. "Sorry! Nothing's wrong—I'm just so excited!" I said when my parents appeared, followed by Wally and Amelia. Everyone looked worried. I could hear Teddy and Pip yelling their little heads off from the dining room, too.

"It's okay, guys!" I yelled back. "Everything's fine!"

"Molly, what in the world—?" Mom started.

"It's a post office sticker!" I said, showing it to Daddy, who had gotten to me first. "This is a thing for when they have a *package* for you at the post office, right?! *Right?!*"

Daddy nodded slowly. Then he handed the thing to Mom, who nodded too.

"So this means there is a *package* for Jess and Rosalie—and holy moly, it could and probably totally *is* from *Jess's dad!*"

Mom pointed out that the note had a date of December 23, which was almost a whole week ago. "Lots of packages go through the post office at this time of year," she said. "I suppose the carrier didn't double-check or send a second note, as would most likely happen normally."

"I am so sure, about seventy-five percent sure, that a package is sitting at the post office in this town, waiting for those two after all this time. And it is full of Christmas happiness!" I kind of yelled.

"Well?" Daddy laughed.

"Well, what?" I laughed back, suddenly not one bit sleepy anymore.

"Well, you'd better get your boots and coat on, Molly Jane Fisher, detective, and get this sticker delivered!"

I got bundled up super fast and ran as fast as I could in the deep snow (which wasn't very fast). I crossed right over Jess's stick-line, walked up their driveway and then knocked and knocked until the door finally opened.

"Molly! Is something wrong?" was Rosalie's first thought and question. "Goodness! Come in!"

I came in and stood on the rug, hoping my snowy boots weren't going to make work and trouble for that nice lady. I shook my head, but that was all I could do while I tried to catch my breath back. It wasn't coming fast enough, and I didn't want to make her wait one more second for the good news. I handed the sticker to her. "The guinea pig . . . Teddy . . . found this, too . . . hide and seek," I gasped. I took a breath and started to feel like normal again. "Fluffy hid it . . . behind . . . the dryer." I took another breath. "It was stuck to this piece of junk mail."

"Oh . . . my. . ." Rosalie had tears in her eyes and her hand over her heart. She read the sticker again and then looked at me. "Oh my," she whispered again. Then she scooped up her kid (who was peeking around her at me) and twirled her all around. "I think we need another trip to town, Jess! This time, we are going to the post office!"

Chapter Twenty-six
Our Last Dinner at Christmas Castle

The rest of the afternoon was super fun. Daddy, Mom, and I found a cool sledding hill. Sledding is something we hardly ever get to do at home, and it was really fun. It was getting dark outside already when we got back, and I was real hungry. It seemed like days ago when I ate those cookies with Daddy, but I would have to wait because dinner wasn't for another hour.

Mom said she wanted to soak in that clawfoot tub again, and Daddy was interested in checking out some football. I only wanted to warm myself up by putting on my pajamas and fuzzy slippers and then sit by the fire and call Nora. I had so much to tell her!

"You were right, you genius, you!" I said. "*P* and *O* was for 'post office.' I think that was the thing Tweets wanted us to know most of all. But it is freaking me out how many other *P*'s and *O*'s there were in the end!"

"Molly, you get yourself into the weirdest stuff."

"I know it."

"Well, you might not even be done with *P* and *O*," Nora said.

"What do you mean by *that*?!"

"Well, Mom told me a person came to our door asking questions about your garage apartment. And guess what his name was?"

"No way."

"Way!"

"What?!"

"His name is . . . Peter Oliver."

"*No!* Nora! No *way!*"

"Molly, what in the world is it with you and your life and your bird?" We laughed together about that amazing stuff. Then I asked about other things and told my best friend how much I was looking forward to seeing her tomorrow.

I could smell dinner, and my stomach started rumbling so much that I think Nora probably heard it too. "I have to have dinner now. I will see you tomorrow afternoon, BFFE&E&E&E&E!"

Nora laughed and said, "Bye, Molly!"

"Dinner!" Rosalie's smile was huge, and she totally hummed while she finished with the table. She dinged the little bell, too, to let us know to come, but we were all there in a flash without needing a reminder. "It's angel hair pasta and sauce with garlic bread and salad. Extra salad for the heroes," she added. Wow, that lady looked like she was the happiest person on the whole earth!

Wally set Teddy and Pip in the travel cage as Rosalie finished up. "Your little friends discovered a missing post office notice for me today," she said in a very happy voice.

"Indeed they did," Wally said. "With much help from our Miss Molly."

"I would like to thank them," she said. "And Molly, too, of course!"

"You already thanked me," I said, but she hugged me again anyway, just like I was her own kid.

She crouched down to look at the guys next. They were very sweet and quiet and both looked at her with those adorable guinea pig eyes of theirs while she talked. "Oh, *thank you*, you sweet little things," Rosalie said. "Thank you *so* much!" She pet each of them for a bit and then stood up straight again. She turned to me and gave me another hug. "Oh, that dog!" she laughed, and when she looked down at me she had happy tears on her face again. "The package from Jim was exactly what Jessie needed to lift her spirits. It was such a difficult Christmas for us this year. But we are having a very happy do-over tonight—thanks to all of you." She wiped at her tears and smiled some more. "Enjoy your final dinner with us. I am off to redo Christmas with my girl!"

Chapter Twenty-seven
Pip is a Rock Star

On the last night, the seven of us sat in the cozy Christmas-y living room by the fire and the pretty tree as Wally finished the Christmas story for us. Daddy fell asleep, but not because it wasn't a good story (it was). He had worn himself out with the sledding, I think.

When the story was done, we sat there for a while, just sitting and being happy that we were together in such a pretty place.

"Thank you all so much," Amelia finally said. "The three of you have made our anniversary celebration so perfect. You are and always will be our dear, dear friends."

Mom said it was definitely a fun time for her, too, relaxing and comfortable, and she didn't need any thanks, actually. "But you're welcome," she added, because you should always say "you're welcome" if someone thanks you.

Wally loaded Teddy and Pip into the carrier super quick before they could start up their complaining, and then they were upstairs. Meanwhile, the rest of the grown-ups started to talk about packing up and going home (not my favorite stuff to hear or talk about).

Amelia gave me a wink. "If you want, you could say good night to the boys. Wally and I will be up in a little bit."

I passed Wally on the way down, and he said the same thing. "I have allowed Pippen the xylophone for a bit," he said with a smile. "Theodore is trying to sleep through it—my poor pal."

I went into the cozy little sitting room. It was dark except for a Christmas tree nightlight and the twinkling tree lights. "Hi, guys," I whispered.

"Hi, Molly Jane," Teddy whispered back. He was snuggled up in his new furry sleeping cozy with his eyes closed.

"Go ahead and sleep, sweetie," I said. "I just wanted to say good night and thank you for all of your help today. You really were, and are, a hero, Teddy. I mean, you found that piece of mail behind the dryer, and that was *exactly* what Rosalie and Jess needed."

Teddy did some purring and said, *"Teddy is very happy to hear that stuff. Hero is good. I like that stuff."*

"What's Pip doing?" I asked. "Did he go to sleep?"

Teddy did a cute little sigh. *"Teddy is not lucky enough for that to be true. Pip is in that igloo doing his thinking about a song. Before that stuff, he was pinking and ponging and tink-tinking on that music machine. The quiet will not last for long. Wait and see."*

The colorful toy xylophone was in a corner with the little hammer next to it. I waited to see what would happen next. It wasn't too long before the little guy peeked out of the igloo.

"Hi, Pip."

"*MOLLY JANE, PIP WRITES A NEW HIT SINGLE. WOULD YOU LIKE TO HEAR?*"

"Very much."

"*IT IS NOT A ROCK SONG, SO FAR, SO IT WILL NOT MAKE THAT TEDDY VERY MAD WHEN HE NEEDS HIS SLEEPING. WE WILL SEE.*"

"I'm ready when you are."

"*Teddy is covering his ears up and not hearing, but only dreaming of quiet times.*"

"*DO NOT BE MAD, MOLLY JANE, BUT THE NAME OF MY NEWEST HIT SINGLE IS 'PIP AND MOM JANE ARE NOT FRIENDS.' HERE IT COMES!*"

A FRIEND IS SOMEONE YOU LIKE—ping!
A FRIEND IS SOMEONE YOU PREFER—pong!
A FRIEND BRINGS TREATS AND IS REAL SWEET
AND A FRIEND DOES NOT MAKE YOU SAY "EEK"
(FOR EXAMPLE)—tink tink!

FRIEND-SHIP IS REAL GOOD—ping!
PIP KNOWS IT LIKE HE SHOULD—pong!
TEDDY IS A FRIEND AND WALLY AND AMELIA
DAD DAN AND EVEN THAT MAX
SOMETIMES—tink tink!

BUT HERE'S THE MYS-TER-Y—ping!
FOR PIPPEN, WHO IS ME (AND FUN TO BE!)—pong!
MOM JANE DID SOMETHING NICE—ping ping!
AND THAT IS MUCH CONFUSING TO ME!—tink tink!

PIP AND MOM JANE ARE NOT FRIENDS
THEY DO NOT PREFER TO BE
IN THE SAME ROOM OR HOUSE OR STREET
OR TOWN, STATE OR COUNT-R-Y

PIP AND MOM JANE ARE NOT FRIENDS—ping ping!
FRIENDS LIKE TO BE CLOSE, YOU SEE—pong!
BUT SHE WAS NICE, INSTEAD OF COLD AS ICE
AND NOW PIP DOES NOT KNOW WHAT WILL BE!—
TINK TINK!

IS IT POS-SI-BLE TO BE—ping ping!
A FRIEND FOR A MOMENT OR THREE?—pong pong!
AND THEN GO BACK TO THE WAY IT WAS
BECAUSE THAT IS WHAT WE'RE BEST AT—TEE
HEE!—tink TINK!!

THE END!

"YES, IT SURELY TAKES PIP MUCH TIME TO DO THAT SONG BECAUSE OF NEEDING TO DO THE MUSIC MACHINE AT THE END OF EVERY PART.

I WILL NEED A HELPER FOR THE ROCK SHOW, AND I THINK IT COULD BE YOU, MOLLY JANE FISHER, IF YOU CAN DO THE MUSIC NOTES AND NOT FREAK OUT ABOUT PIP'S MANY SCREAMING FANS. THANK YOU."

I pet Pip and smiled into his cute little face. "Okay. I'll help any way I can. And you know what? I totally get it, about you and my mom. I have the same deal with Benny Nubb, like I said before. I think the important thing is that you give her—and I give him—a break and a chance when it's possible. Now we know that they *can* be nice, and maybe they want to be. It takes some time and practice, that's all."

"MAYBE."

"Are you sleepy yet?"

"MAYBE."

"It was a big day. The song was great, by the way. And I'm not mad about the title. Don't worry. Sleep well, little Pip. I love you!"

"MOLLY JANE, YOU ARE A FRIEND, FOR SURE AND FOR ALL THE TIMES. PIP LOVES YOU BACK. PIP AND MOLLY JANE ARE SURELY FRIENDS."

Chapter Twenty-eight
Heading Home

"I have wonderful news!" Amelia, Mom, and I were sitting at the dining room table having muffins and cheesy eggs. Wally and Daddy had the not-fun job of making the suitcases and stuff pile up sadly by the front door. "I have found Elizabeth Danby!"

Mom said, "Really?"

And I said, "Oh my gosh! That was so fast!"

"Well, she wasn't actually hard to find. It turns out that she is a rather high-profile person with her own business, and she lives right in New York City!"

"What business is she in?" Mom asked.

"She is an interior designer." Amelia turned to me and explained, "That means she decorates houses." She looked around her at the pretty house we were in and said, "Which makes sense."

"I think living here would make anyone good at decorating," I agreed.

"Anyway, she says she is more than happy to look up my sister and make up for the many years of missed opportunities. I am so pleased!"

"That's great news, Amelia," I said.

"Thanks to Molly."

"And Teddy and Pip. And Daddy."

"Thanks to all of you!" Amelia laughed. "You boys have done a *lot* of good for the humans around you these past few days," she said, turning to look at Teddy and Pip.

But they just kept on munching their morning salad and didn't say anything back about that. They were a little grumpy, even though they were wearing their blue and white jingle hats (which were totally cute). They knew a long car ride was coming. They do not like long car rides. Or any car rides, actually.

"I am going to pop the two old letters into the mail as soon as I get back," Amelia went on. "I will include a note for each of the friends about how the letters were found. I will also give them phone numbers and addresses, and then we shall see what happens next."

The back door opened, and Amelia did a "shh!" at Teddy and Pip, even though they weren't talking one bit this morning. "Rosalie?" she called.

Our cook and caretaker peeked into the dining room and gave us a big smile. "I wanted to say goodbye and thank you, again, for finding our note about the package," she said.

"You're welcome," I said. "I was super happy to find that thing!"

She handed me a big brown envelope. "This is for Jessie's new grandmas."

"Wow! She's fast! Don't worry, I will make sure they get these, like, tomorrow. They won't get lost, for sure. We don't have a dog, and my bird might chew one of them, but he can't carry even one letter in his little beak."

Rosalie laughed a little about that.

"I'll help the grandmas to get letters back to Jess, too, as soon as possible," I promised. "Maybe we'll have an After-New-Year's party all about letter writing."

"Wonderful." She crouched down to look at Teddy and Pip next. "I love your hats," she said. Then she tickled each of them under the chin. "Thank you again," she said to them. "So much."

She stood up again and smoothed at her hair. "You know what? I have a feeling that life is going to be a whole lot happier around here, now that we've met all of you."

What can a person say about that? Wow, right? We all just sat there, smiling kind of a lot.

"Well, I will let you go now. Just leave the keys on the counter when you go. No need to lock up. And please say you'll come back soon," Rosalie said. "You are always welcome here."

Epilogue

"Yeah, he tapped those two letters, like, a lot," Max yawned. "Over and over until I was thinking maybe I should get him to a little birdie doctor. Or whatever. For his beak."

"Your beak's okay, isn't it?" I said as I gave Tweets a kiss on that busy little warm beak. "You are amazing," I said to him. "How in the world did you know about all that stuff going on three hours away from here?"

"I dunno, Mol," Max said with a little "I don't buy it" smile. "I think it's coincidence."

I shook my head at that guy. "Is it a coincidence that the man who wants to rent our garage apartment is named Peter Oliver?"

Max stopped smiling and yawning and looked pretty shocked about that. "Uh . . . well, I dunno," he said. "But . . ."

"I think there's another mystery coming, and it's all about that guy. You just wait and see!"

"Okay, Mol. I'll wait and see. But if I can give you some advice, maybe stay out of it, even if the guy has a mystery around him. Bizarro stuff always happens around you. Maybe for once, you can keep away from it."

"Well, that guy might not even be our renter. I mean, Mom has to talk to him and decide if he is the right person." I did a shrug.

"Let's hope she decides he isn't, and she rents to someone named John Smith instead."

I shook my head at him and said, "Well, you are done bird-sitting, so you can go get lots of rest. Have a nice long nap, Max."

"You're welcome for the bird-sitting. I'm sure you meant to say thank you, right?"

I gave my goofy cousin a big hug (with Tweets on my head, which was weird). "Thank you!" I said real loud.

"Alright. Alright. Let's get Mr. Feathers back in his home sweet home so you can take him back to yours."

I tucked Tweets into his cage and locked the door as Mom and Aunt Patty walked in. Mom said she wanted to get going back to our house.

"I have the car all warmed up," she said. "Put the blanket over the bird and let's go."

"Okay. Thanks again, Max. And Aunt Patty," I added, because I had an idea that maybe she did most of the work.

"MAX IS COOL!"

I pulled the blanket back off and stared at my bird. "Tweets? What in the world did you just *say*?"

"HELLO PRETTY! BIRDIE BIRDIE BIRDIE!"

"Right. That's what I thought. Okay, well, see you guys!" I called, because Max had disappeared, probably to the room with the biggest TV.

P.S.

Christmas Miracles
1. *Benny Nubb shows up at the party with Frank.*
2. *I felt sorry for Scary Evelyn.*
3. *Evelyn and Elizabeth maybe will be friends again after twenty-five years.*
4. *Mom holding Pip. Whoa!*
5. *Mom scratching Pip behind his ears.*
6. *Pip being quiet while Mom did those things.*
7. *Finding the letters.*
8. *Finding the post office package sticker!*

PIP'S HIT SINGLES

PIP IS NOT A BABY

Pip is not a baby.
Pip rocks and rocks and ROCKS!!
Pip is not a baby in a crib!
Pip is not a baby.
Pip does not cry.
Pip is a dude.
Pip is a tough guy!

Baby sacks are not for a dude like Pip
And maybe they are not for Teddy, too.
Or either.
Pip is a tough guy, who does not ever cry,
and baby sacks are the worst of times!
No good!!
The end.

PIP WANTS A TREAT

Pip is me—and a treat will be
The way to solve a mys-ter-y!
Pip is me—and "no treat" means we
Won't catch a bad guy—NO-SIR-EE!

FINDING TREATS

Finding treats in a
Haunted house bedroom
Sneaky sneaking round and round.
Molly Jane hides them,
Pip and Teddy find them—
Best and worst of times all in one!
CRUNCH!

Finding treats in a

Haunted house bedroom
Sneaky sneaking round and round.
Lettuce (YUM!), broccoli (YUM!)
And carrots, too (YUM YUM)!
Best and worst of times all in one!
CRUNCH!

FINDING TREATS TWO

Finding treats in a
Haunted house downstairs
Sneaky sneaking round and round.
Molly Jane hides them,
Pip and Teddy find them—
Best and worst of times all in one!
CRUNCH!

Finding treats in a
Haunted house downstairs
Sneaky sneaking round and round.
Lettuce (YUM!), broccoli (YUM!)
And carrots, too (YUM YUM)!
Best and worst of times all in one!
CRUNCH!

PIP AND MOM JANE ARE NOT FRIENDS

A FRIEND IS SOMEONE YOU LIKE—ping!
A FRIEND IS SOMEONE YOU PREFER—pong!
A FRIEND BRINGS TREATS AND IS REAL SWEET
AND A FRIEND DOES NOT MAKE YOU SAY 'EEK'
(FOR EXAMPLE)—tink tink!

FRIEND-SHIP IS REAL GOOD—ping!
PIP KNOWS IT LIKE HE SHOULD—pong!
TEDDY IS A FRIEND AND WALLY AND AMELIA
DAD DAN AND EVEN THAT MAX
SOMETIMES—tink tink!

BUT HERE'S THE MYS-TER-Y—ping!
FOR PIPPEN, WHO IS ME (AND FUN TO BE!)—pong!
MOM JANE DID SOMETHING NICE—ping ping!
AND THAT IS MUCH CONFUSING TO ME!—tink tink!

PIP AND MOM JANE ARE NOT FRIENDS
THEY DO NOT PREFER TO BE
IN THE SAME ROOM OR HOUSE OR STREET
OR TOWN, STATE OR COUNT-R-Y

PIP AND MOM JANE ARE NOT FRIENDS—ping ping!
FRIENDS LIKE TO BE CLOSE, YOU SEE—pong!
BUT SHE WAS NICE, INSTEAD OF COLD AS ICE
AND NOW PIP DOES NOT KNOW WHAT WILL BE!—
TINK TINK!

IS IT POS-SI-BLE TO BE—ping ping!
A FRIEND FOR A MOMENT OR THREE?—pong pong!
AND THEN GO BACK TO THE WAY IT WAS
BECAUSE THAT IS WHAT WE'RE BEST AT—TEE
HEE!—tink TINK!!

THE END!

BEST FRIENDS CLUB
(as of December 2017)

HUMANS
Wally•Amelia•Molly Jane•Dad•Bill•Lisa•Allison•
Mia•Alexandria•Nancy•Jennah•Terri•Bella•Sophia•
Sam•Cally•Jessamine•Jake•Mackenzie•Seth•
Alexandra•Chantal•Isaac•Goldie•Ruth•Rose•Lenny•
Annie•Benjamin•Ryann•Emilyn•Hannah•Eric•Aidan•
Amber•Grace•Chloe•Vahishta•Lily•MollyAnn•Darren•
Dylan•Logan•Abby•Bella•Mckayla•Hannah•Maggie•
Patterson's First Grade Class•Ruth•Sofie•Calli•Lizzie•
Kayla•Kaylee•Joanna (and family)•Gwen•Ally•
Alexandrea•Vahishta•Claire•Matthew•Rachael•Ally•
Sue•Alex•Henry•Hannah•Sasha•Estela•Samantha•
Erin•Quinn•Julia•Emma•Anna•Clara•Ruby•Marina•
Brandi•Miss Hodis and Room E-1•Emma•Celeste•
•Delton•Bree•Hayden•Kayden•Layla•Gwen•Sam•
Emma•Catie•Delaney•Elise•Katie•Kyleigh•Lily•Loklo•
Roro•Kokomo•Sebastian•Sylvia•Milly•Owen•Leona
•Sarah•Ella•Lilly•Mallory•Kyle•Trevor•Kevin•Carla•
Sarah

GUINEA PIGS
Teddy•Pip•Maggie•Peanut•Mimi•Miranda•Coco•
Magic•Muffin•Nugget•Squeak•Hershey•Butterscotch•
Ormsby•Pedrosa•Chestnut•Mocha•Scamp•LiL Betty•
Angelstunky•Squeakersiren•Gizmo•Princess•Pearl•
Cinnamon•Sugar•Fuzzy•Spice•Peruvian•Linniea
Serena Silkie•Fuzzcake•Pipsqueak•Molly•Rosie•
Babooshka•Little Fussy•S'mores•Sparkle•Bevo•
Ranger•Oreo•Freckles•Cappy•Ginger•Pumpkin•
Twinkie•Ginger•Piko•Lola•Lotta•Butterscotch•

Stanley•Mr. Pickles•Oreo•Chewy•Stripes•Snowball•
Jilly Boo•PeeWee•Pipsqueak•Teddy•Dalmation•
Skippy•Linny•Snickers•Romeo•Juliet•Alexander•
Angel•Chester (Mr. Awesome)•Squeakers•Princess•
Junior•Marshmallow•Mischief•Herb•Chanel•Magic•
Cream•Willow•Zuna•Sadie•Autumn•Malena•
Swift•Tom•Caramel Chip•Rosie•Fluffy•Cupcake•
Zippy•Mr. Two Shoes•Howard•Oreo•Kit-Kat•Mavis•
Molly•Moose•Chi•Kiy•Sammie•Calico•Junior•Curly•
Playdo•Caramel•Butterscotch•Magic•Snowflake•
Pinkieshy•Fuzzcake•Blackie•Buttercup•Lilac•
Dandelion Leaf•George•Zeke•Heidi•Holly•Fraya•
Xavyr•Talia•Pandora•Brownie•Inky•Flicker•Flower•
Mouse•Ace•Peanut•Oreo•Snicker Doodle•
Cookie Dough•Mocha•Lovie•Gus•Charlie•Peanut
Butter•Chocolate•Midnight•Jack•Arthas•Gina•
Phoebe•Pandora•Talia•Bitsy•Jolie•Smore•Kiwi•
Butterscotch•Cleo•Chai•Iggy•Oreo (a.k.a. Momma
Pig)•Flopsy•Mops•Cheeks•ButterPop•Beany•Cocoa•
Teddy•Popcorn•LoveBug•Crested•CJ•Babs•Browny•
Chewy•Bubbles•Fluffy•Marshmallow•Bubbles•Harry•
Calvin•Speedy•Luna•Odin•Artemis•Zeus•Hermionie•
Galaxy•Pumpkin•Honey•Spotty•Fluffy•Honeay•
Snowy•Freddie•Wicket•Chiclet•Nutmeg•Jessie•
Summer Sunshine•Annabeth•Linus•Lucy•Honey•
Solomon•Enoch

Can you find your name and your guinea pigs on the Best
Friends Club list?

(Sign up on the website to be in the Best Friends Club!)

For more fun with Teddy and Pip, go to

www.teddyandpip.com

Made in the USA
Monee, IL
13 September 2021